I0658360

BLOODY MONEY BAGS

VIOLENT LOVE

KINGPEN

LOCK DOWN PUBLICATIONS AND CA$H PRESENTS

First Edition 2024

Printed in the United States of America

Lock Down Publications

P.O. Box 944

Stockbridge, GA 30281

www.lockdownpublications.com

Like our page on Facebook: Lock Down Publications

www.facebook.com/lockdownpublications.ldp

STAY CONNECTED WITH US!

Text **LOCKDOWN** to 22828 to stay up-to-date with new releases, sneak peaks, contests and more…

Like our page on Facebook:
Lock Down Publications

Join Lock Down Publications/The New Era Reading Group

Visit our website:
www.lockdownpublications.com

Follow us on Instagram:
Lock Down Publications

Email Us: We want to hear from you!

1

ANGEL

I stared at myself in the mirror as I applied another coat of eye shadow to my left eye. I looked at my reflection in the mirror. The vanity mirror that my so-called loving husband bought me for our one-year anniversary. I once told myself that I would never be one of them women. One that lets a man put his hands on me. Looking at my reflection in the mirror, my black eye called me a liar.

Ken, my husband of two years, stirred in his sleep. He lay in our bed naked, except for the silk sheets that covered his ass and man parts. He opened his eyes and watched me put on my make-up.

"Where you going?" Ken asked as he picked up a half-empty bottle of Bud Light that he had left over from the night before. Ken took the bottle to the head. It was full. He belched loudly as soon as he finished. I shook my head in disgust as he tried to sit the empty bottle on the nightstand, but it ended up falling to the all-white plush carpet.

Ken stumbled behind me as I applied my make-up. He placed his hand on my shoulder. I don't know exactly why, but my eyes closed on their own, and my breath got caught in my lungs as my body tensed up. I can recall when his touch used to make me feel alive. His touch would make me melt under his fingertips like a stick of butter. But now, I despise it.

"Don't forget to take my lawyer his fee," Ken said as he raised his hand from my shoulder. I opened my eyes and watched him through the mirror walk back to the bed. I stared a hole in his back the entire short distance.

"That's on the agenda too," I said as I closed my eye shadow case. Ken flopped on the bed flat on his belly; his bare ass was in the air. I stared at him as he lightly snored. When he was drunk, he did two things at lightning speed: have sex, and go to sleep. I looked at him through the mirror as he scratched his ass, then rolled over onto his side. I turned my head in disgust. I wasn't the woman I always thought I was, and he definitely wasn't the man I fell in love with three years ago.

———

'*AY THAT MUSCLE truck sit tall as fuck / It's so big can't even tow it / Don't like snakes, keep my grass cut so low can't even mow it*'. Rocko's "U.O.E.N.O" blared through the loudspeakers at *V-Live* strip club in Houston.

I smacked my lips, slicking on my lip gloss. I double checked my appearance to make sure I was up to par. I had to be on my best shit tonight, because Big Ken and the Bloody Money Bagg clique were supposed to come through. I had never met Big Ken personally, but my home-girl, Sparkle, told me that the last time he came through with his clique, they made it rain all night. I wasn't no fool; I missed out the last time, not again.

I stormed out of the dressing room onto the main floor. The club was packed way over capacity. Bodies were everywhere. Almost all the men in the club wore black and red B.M.B shirts, and the women wore practically nothing. I wasn't a regular worker at *V-Live*; my main club was *Temptations* in Fort Worth. But I would venture to other strip clubs, depending on the clientele.

I looked around at all the money that was stuck to the floor, as well as the sweaty strippers' bodies. Since I wasn't a regular, I would always find me one good trick, or a table full of dudes that either had money, or looked like they had money, and prayed that they would spend every dime on me. As I danced by myself, I made my ass cheeks jump one cheek at a time doing my best to catch someone's eye. I didn't have a big derrière; my ass was very grippable though. I knew a lot of strippers that got their ass done or had fat taken out of their stomach to make their waist look smaller, but I didn't choose to do that. I kept my body the way my mama gave it to me. And even then, I twerked harder than every bitch in the room. I did it for chicks like me. I did it to send out a reminder. Little booties mattered!

Lost in my dance, a hand clamped on my arm, killing my vibe instantly. I spun around, ready to glare daggers, but my scowl melted away. A handsome dark-skinned man stood before me, his diamond teeth flashing brilliantly under the club lights.

"Damn, did I do something wrong?" I asked him as I

looked at his appearance. The man wore a B.M.B diamond chain, but unlike everyone else, he didn't have on one of the B.M.B matching shirts.

"My bad, shorty. I was just tryna get a dance from you, is all. I saw how you was in yo' own world, and I wanted to be a part of it," he smoothly said.

As he stared at me, I stood on my back legs, making my ass pop out more for his enjoyment, as well as mine. I was really enjoying how he was staring at me. I turned to the side shyly and gave him a full view of what he would be spending his money on, if he played his cards right. "Dances aren't free, you know."

He smiled and made my pun-pun soaking wet. He pulled me by my hand towards the V.I.P section. He was so sexy; I didn't care where he dragged me off to. I was going to follow him. The V.I.P section was blocked off with a velvet rope. The V.I.P section had more than twenty B.M.B members present; all of them held expensive bottles of liquor, and champagne. There was money all over the couches and floor as a group of strippers threw themselves into their routines, vying for the biggest cut. They were filming each other as they made it rain all over the club. My admirer sat down and pulled me onto his lap. I positioned myself directly over his dick and slowly started to grind on him. As I started to get a rhythm, he held my waist on both sides, stopping me.

"Wait, shorty," he said.

I looked back at him confused. "What? I thought you wanted a dance?"

"I only said that to get you to come with me."

"Look, you're cute, but my time is money. I don't conversate, or dance for free," I said, as serious as a heart attack.

"I feel you, shorty. Trust me, if money is all you want, then that isn't a problem. I'mma hustla, so I respect the hustle!" he said as he pulled a fat knot of money from his pocket. The whole time I was grinding on his dick, I was thinking he had a fat dick, but I thought wrong. He handed me the whole roll of money and said, "Take whatever you feel is worth your time."

I was stuck. Never ever has a man gave me all of his money and told me to take what I wanted. "Boy! You better stop playing with me. I'll keep this whole stack." I laughed it off, but I was *dead ass*!

He laughed at me and said, "Keep it."

"I can't keep all of your money."

"All of my money," he said, then laughed. He patted my leg, indicating he wanted me to stand up. I stood to the side. He leaned down and grabbed a Louis Vuitton duffle bag. He unzipped it, then opened it for me to see inside. Inside were blocks of rubber band money, along with a money shooter. "This is the definition of B.M.B.," he said, standing up.

"You work for Big Ken?" I asked as he loaded up the money shooter with a stack of hundreds.

He laughed at me like I was a stand-up comedian. "Work for Big Ken," he laughed again. "I am *Big Ken*," he said as he handed me the gun loaded with hundred-dollar bills. Big Ken pulled his shirt over his head. The only thing he wore over his chest was a big diamond encrusted chain that had the words: *B.M.B*, and another chain that said, *Big Ken*.

I looked at him dumbfounded. The whole time I was dissing him, talking about chasing a bag, and the entire time I was sitting right on top of the bag. Big Ken turned my back to him as he stood behind me. "You know how to use one of these, don't you?" He helped me with the money shooter as if he was teaching me to play baseball.

"Actually, I don't. I've never been on this side of the gun, only the opposite," I said.

Big Ken stood closely behind me and said, "Look how the tables have turned." His words made me blush.

"Wait, why am I pointing this towards the dance floor? Shouldn't I be pointing it in here?"

"Why would you want to shoot the money in here?" he asked.

"That way, once I'm finished, I can get the majority of it."

"Shorty, calm down. Money isn't everything," he said, sounding a little disappointed.

I looked over my shoulder at him and said, "Says the man that throws it around at his disposal."

"I do this to give back. Instead of passing out turkeys, I give cash."

"Exactly. That's why I'm tryna get some." I laughed.

"What's your name?"

"Angel." I normally would say my stripper name, which was Lady Twix, but the vibe he gave me made me tell him my real name.

"Angel, huh? It fits you perfect." His words made me smile. He was a charmer.

"Did your mama name you Big Ken?"

"Nah. Actually, my real name is Kendrick. My uncle gave me the nick name, *Big Ken.*" As he talked, he emptied the money shooter, spreading hundred-dollar bills all around the club. The money was still falling as he refilled the money shooter like money grew on trees. Before I knew it, we both made it rain dead presidents all over the club. I was having so much fun, I wasn't thinking about all the time I was wasting with him, until he said, "The rest of that is yours, for your time." He picked the duffle up and pulled out three blocks of hundreds, then he handed it to me.

"Wow, Big Ken, this is a helluva lot of money. At least let me give you a dance." If he thought I was going to be prideful and give the money back, he had the wrong bitch.

"I'm cool on the dance, ma."

I looked at him sideways and said, "Wait, hol' up! If you think I'm going to sleep with you for all of this bread, you better rethink it."

He put his hands up in surrender and laughed. "It ain't even like that, shorty, trust me."

"Then what is it like then?" I surely wanted to hear this.

"Someone as beautiful as you shouldn't have to shake yo' ass to make som' cash. I know some chicks use the excuse of them strippin' as they're doing it to get money for school. So, I'm goin' to give you a way out, and you can keep whatever reason you're strippin' to yo'self."

I laughed. "I didn't have an excuse. And who says I want a way out? Who says I don't enjoy shakin' my ass?"

"There's more to life, shit that you haven't seen yet."

"And you're going to show me?"

"That's if you'll let me."

"You don't even know me."

"We got the rest of our lives to get to know each other." His words were what did it for me. That same day we exchanged numbers. Three months later, I moved into his house, and a year later, we said *I do*. And now, I wish I never met him.

2

EMMANUEL

I snatched my reading glasses off my face, tossing them onto my desk. I rubbed my temple as I looked over my latest case. The United States versus Kendrick Watson. My office door cracked open, catching my attention. Janice, my secretary of two years, stuck her head inside.

"Manny, would you like some coffee or cappuccino?"

"Coffee would be nice," I said as my smart watch went off. I looked at the small screen as *Happy Anniversary* popped up continuously on the screen. I jumped from my seat in a panic.

"Janice!" I yelled as loud as I could. Janice ran inside of my office wondering what was going on.

"Yes," she said, wide-eyed.

"Please, tell me today's not December the third." I was praying deep down that it wasn't. That somehow, the date on my watch was wrong. Or, that I set the alarm on the wrong year.

Janice tap'd her smartwatch to bring the screen alive.

"Yes, today is the third of December. Why?" As soon as she asked the question, she covered her mouth with her hand.

Exactly! I thought to myself. I hurried and stacked all of my paperwork in my briefcase along with my MacBook pro.

"Order me two dozen roses from Walmart, have it ready for pickup," I said as I rushed out the door past her. I shook my head. I couldn't believe I forgot my anniversary, again.

———

I LET OUT a sigh of relief as I pulled up to the house to find the driveway empty of Hannah's car. That would only mean I beat her home. Which meant I had time to set everything up for a beautiful night. I walked in the front door. Our pug dog that Hannah named after herself ran to the door, excited to see me. I shooed her away as I hurried to the living room.

"First things first, rose petals," I said out loud to myself as I started peeling roses from their stems. I started making a trail from the front door, up the stairs to our bedroom. As I walked in the bedroom, I noticed the shower was on in the bathroom, but the door was closed. Steam rushed from the small crack at the bottom of the door. I smiled as I heard soft passionate moans from my wife. My first thought was that she was pleasing herself thinking of me. It had been close to two months since the last time we were intimate. It wasn't that I didn't find my beautiful wife attractive; God knows she's the apple of my eye. Her chinky-eyed butt drives me up the wall. The problem is, I stay super busy with work. Most days I work myself up to my elbows, and have to pull all-nighters. And sometimes I work until the next morning. She has been telling me things have got to change. And I couldn't agree more. And I will, starting tonight. I stripped down to my birthday suit, stroking myself at the same time to get myself ready. I smiled as I stepped out of my clothes. I placed my hand on the door knob. I was dying on the inside to feel her in my arms. I opened the bathroom as quietly as possible. The room was filled with steam, making it hard to see. Hannah's moans became louder behind the closed shower curtain. I held a bouquet of roses in my left hand, and my hard dick in my right hand. I slowly peeled the shower curtain back with a huge smile on my face.

My dick instantly became soft, and my smile disappeared as I stared at my wife getting fucked hard from the back by my best friend—Caesar. Neither noticed that I had entered their affair, until I gasped loudly. They both looked to the side. All that could be heard was a popping sound as Caesar's dick slipped from my wife's wet pussy.

Caesar, or—as I called him—Lil' C, which was the name I gave him in college. Caesar looked like a deer caught in headlights. Hannah's eyes went down to my soft dick. She looked at it with pity. I don't know what got into me, but I started swinging the roses as if they were a baseball bat. As I went from Caesar to Hannah, the roses turned into rose stems. Caesar shoved me backwards as he ran out the bathroom. I ran behind him, chasing him, then a thought came to mind. I ran over to my nightstand and grabbed my lock box with my gun inside. "Manny, no!"

Hannah screamed. She wasn't no fool. She knew what I was about to do.

I cocked my 9mm back and ran down the stairs two at a time. As I made it outside, I looked around for my so-called best friend. I couldn't believe him. We grew up together. We were frat brothers, even college roommates. Now, we seemed to have shared the same woman.

As I looked around, my garage door opened, Caesar's Dodge pickup sped out, and passed me. I aimed my gun and fired off round after round into his back windshield. Did I hit him? Hell, I don't know, but Lord knows I tried. The way he turned the corner, I doubt if I did.

I stood in my driveway with my gun in hand. I was completely nude, and aggravated. My nosey ass neighbor stood in her grass with her cellphone in her hand. I didn't know if she planned on recording me, or calling the cops. I ran back inside before she was able to make up her mind.

I ran back upstairs the same way I ran down them, two at a time. I stormed inside our bedroom. Hannah stood at the foot of the bed in her pink plush robe. Her hair was slick from the shower. She still looked amazing, even behind the disgust I tried to paint over her.

"Did you kill him?" she asked as she laid some of her clothes on the bed to pack.

I shook my head. "No. But I damn sure tried."

She smiled. "Manny, I'm leaving you," she said.

Obviously! I know she didn't think she was staying after the stunt she just pulled. I know our marriage vows said, *for better or worse*. But fucking my best friend on our anniversary day was the worst it could get. "Why, Hannah?" I asked. I asked the question, but on the inside I didn't know why I wanted an explanation. Maybe it was the man in me. She had hurt my pride. I felt like getting an explanation was my way of rebuilding my pride for the next woman.

"Manny, we've been over for a long time now. You haven't acknowledged me for months!" she said as she continued to toss clothes on the bed.

"So, where do you think you're going?"

"I don't know. I'll stay at a hotel, or rent an apartment!" she said as she looked around for more clothes to pack.

"I meant, with all of that. You can go, but you're not taking anything I bought you." I don't know what she thought this was. I was like Quavo when it came to giving gifts. As a man giveth, so a man can taketh away.

Hannah laughed. "So childish." She shoved the suitcase she was filling to the side. She grabbed the keys to her Mercedes Benz. The Mercedes Benz I bought her.

"Keys, too!" I said.

She huffed and tossed the keys at my feet. "I'll see you in court," she spat.

"And I'll see you to the door."

3

EMMANUEL

Three Days Later

"Mhmmmm!" I stirred in my sleep. "Don't try to woo me now, Hannah. Ohhh! That-that's my, spot. Stop, Hannah, I'm not going to take you back."

Woof! Woof! Hannah, the dog, licked the side of my face, awakening me from my drunken sleep.

"Okay, Hannah. Okay, I'm up." She jumped all over me as I sat my back against the couch. I rubbed my eyes and looked around.

I was in the movie room, the movie room that Hannah took so much pride in having. Yet, she left it all behind. The movie projector was playing our wedding day on the screen. I looked down at my new best friend, then I picked him up. Me and Jack Daniels looked at the screen as we listened to Hannah lie with a straight face.

'*Emmanuel, my loving, fantastic, better half. I love you so much. Words can't describe how you make me feel.*

Everything about you is a gift from God. It's like as soon as words leave your mouth, your words come from God. Your vibe is heavenly. You control me in ways I wouldn't understand. The way you can make my heart beat out of its chest, then one second later, place it back and calm it down with soothing words. I will never forget how you chased me around the mall that day. I thought it was weird, then it seemed romantic. Now that you've caught me, I pray that you never let me go. I loved you yesterday. I love you today. And, I'll love you forever.'

"Pshhh! I guess forever came fast, huh, Jack?" My words slurred as I took a sip from my new best friend.

My cell started ringing from inside my pocket. I dug in my pocket and pulled it out. "Hello!" I spoke into the phone. No one said anything. I looked at the screen, then laughed at myself. "You're drunk!" I said to myself as I noticed I was talking to my alarm.

Woof! Woof! Woof! Hannah barked at me as she chased her tail in circles. I learned over the years that that meant she was hungry.

Woof! Woof! Hannah continued to bark. "Okay, I'm getting up now." I used the couch for support. Hannah jumped up on her hind legs. I picked up my new best friend. "No man gets left behind, Jack. You know why you're my new best friend. Because you, you make all the pain go away. And—you'll never sleep with my wife. Ex! Ex-wife, that is." I spoke to Jack as we maneuvered through the house.

There was broken glass everywhere. Pictures of Hannah had magically fallen from the wall. Somehow, the picture that had me and Hannah in them only had me in them now. As I made it to the kitchen without getting any glass in my feet, I grabbed Hannah's dog bowl and filled it with her food. Then I grabbed a raw egg from the refrigerator and cracked it over her food. As soon as I sat the bowl down, Hannah started scoffing her food down, while out of the corner of her eyes she was staring me down.

I kept my best friend company as I walked upstairs to my bedroom. I hadn't been inside the room since the day I caught my wife and best friend exploring each other's insides. Ex-best friend, that is. I sighed as I cracked the bedroom door open. I stood at the door as if there was a ghost inside keeping me from going inside. I finally gained enough courage to go inside. The room was exactly like she left it. Her half-filled luggage was still on the bed. As soon as I saw it, the anger inside of me rose. I swiped the luggage to the floor, making a mess in the process. I sat at the foot of the bed, the same spot where her luggage had just been. The luggage she was using to leave me. I placed my face in my hands and cried.

How could I let this happen? My wife, and my best friend. Ex-wife and ex-best friend, that is. My mind went back to how Lil' C. No, I take that back, I can never call him Lil' C anymore; he's Caesar. Better yet, he's Brutus. A backstabber. A manipulator. A disgrace of a great name. But again, my mind went back to them, in the shower. Her moans, his tight eyes as he stroked something that didn't belong to him; yet, at that moment, he possessed it. The look she gave me once she noticed I was there. Like I was interrupting something that she so desperately needed to take care of. Like I had crashed a party that I wasn't invited to. And come to think about it, I can't recall if they wore a condom or not.

I shook my head in disgust. I stood up and stared at the bed. I closed my eyes as I snatched the bed spread off. I slowly opened my eyes, afraid of what I might see. And my fear had showed its face. It came in an image of cum stains. I threw my new best friend at the wall. I was better off alone. I sat down back at the foot of the bed, away from the cum stains. I let the tears fall as I placed my face back in my hands. Hannah the dog licked my hands and barked. I looked up at her and smiled. "Yeah, fuck that bitch!"

———

I PULLED up to my office and parked my F-250 in my private parking spot. I decided to get some work done to keep them cheating bastards off my mind. I stepped out of my truck with my Tom Ford shades on. The sun was beginning to hide from the world, but I kept my glasses to hide my late night drinking session from everyone else. I tried staying at home, but everything I saw reminded me of her. So, I decided to go to work to clear my head. As I walked up to my building, the Dallas sun violated my privacy. My forehead started sweating instantly. I knew it was really the liquor running out of my pores.

I retrieved my keys from my pocket and placed them in the lock. A shadow shielded the light from behind me. I looked through the glass to see who was behind me. "Are you Mr. Stevens?" a soft voice said from behind me.

I turned to see a beautiful, young, short African-American woman. The lady wore a pair of all-white shorts, with an all-white Gucci shirt to match. Over her eyes were a pair of white and black Gucci shades. As I saw the frames, I wondered if she wore hers for the same purpose as I wore mine. "Yes, I'm Mr. Stevens. How may I help you?" I unlocked the front door and stepped to the side so that she could enter first. I stepped in behind her and hit the light switch.

"My name is Angel Watson. My husband's name is Kendrick Watson."

I nodded and said, "I see. And, he sent you to?"

"He sent me to give you his payment. But, I also have a few questions of my own." We walked into my office. She took a seat on the opposite side of my oak wood desk.

I took a seat in my big leather chair that I bought for moments just like this one. To feel important. Needed. "I can answer simple questions, with only simple answers. As far as questions concerning his case, I can only answer questions to the person whose name is on my check."

Mrs. Watson nodded. She looked to be in a deep thought. "Client-lawyer privilege. I understand," she said.

I smiled and said, "So, ask away."

"Okay. So, I wanted to ask you, could you really keep my husband out of prison?"

I sat up in my chair. "If you don't know, he's paying me almost a hundred grand to do just that. I am being paid to do my job, and I will do my job to my fullest extent."

She nodded. "I like that," she said standing up. "So, whenever you're ready."

"Ready for what exactly?"

"I know you didn't expect me to drive with, as you say, close to a hundred grand here by my lonesome." She showed me a very beautiful smile. I can imagine it was most likely the same smile she gave Mr. Watson so he could place the huge diamond she had on her finger.

"I only take checks or money orders."

"Mr. Stevens. With you being my husband's lawyer, I know you already know he's being charged with kingpin charges, as well as organized crimes. Being that you've already spoken with him before, you have to know what's true, and what's not true. With that being said, the feds have seized all of his assets and accounts. So, a check will not be an option. And I know you don't expect me to take ninety-five thousand dollars to a corner store, and have them make it into a money order. So, our only option is cash."

"I've never taken that much cash from a client before. But, I know how things can get with the feds. So, I'll make an exception this once." I stood up and said, "Where do you have to go to get it?"

"It's not too far away. A short drive, it won't take long to get there." I stared at her petite body as she walked off. It had been over ten years since I had a black woman. Being that she was my client's wife, I would have to wait even longer.

I grabbed my keys and turned the lights off. As we walked out the front door, I locked the door behind us. The sun had finally deserted the sky, and the moon had taken its place. I walked up beside Angel as she stood beside a pink and white Porsche.

"I'll follow you there," I said.

Angel showed me her signature smile and said, "Don't be silly. Get in. You can keep me company during the drive." She opened her door and got inside. As she brought the silent engine to life, she reached across the console and opened up the passenger door for me. I walked around the expensive car and sat in the passenger seat. I huffed under my breath as I put my seat belt on. For some odd reason, I felt as if I was doing something that I had no business doing. Yet, the thought of ninety-five thousand dollars in cash seemed too good to be true.

Angel pulled out the lot, and at the same time, she turned her radio up just a tad. A song by Megan Thee Stallion and Cardi B was playing. Cardi B was rapping about her having some wet ass pussy. I shook my head as Angel rapped the song as if she was the one that wrote it. I wasn't a big fan of gangsta rap, although I did sometimes listen to the old Young Jeezy albums. But I could never get into listening to someone speak about how wet their private parts were.

I looked outside the window as the suburbs turned into the projects. I looked to the side at Angel. She turned the radio up, blocking out whatever it was I was about to say. I looked out the window again and shook my head. An old quote came to mind. 'All money ain't good money.'

———

WE ARRIVED in Oak Cliff at a section eight project housing called, *The Browns*. As we drove through the apartments, all eyes were glued on Angel's Porsche. Cardi B was no longer playing, but Megan Thee Stallion was on, and this time she wasn't speaking on how wet her pussy was. This time, she was speaking on how someone was a bitch. Angel finally turned the radio down. Whatever I was going to say, I kept it to myself. My only concern now was to make it out of the projects with the money we came for.

Angel parked in front of an apartment building and turned the car off. I stayed seated as she opened her car door. She grabbed her purse, then she looked back at me. "Let's go. We'll be in, and out. I promise."

I sighed as I took my seat belt off. As bad as I wanted to stay my black ass in the car, I felt that I was safer with her. I stepped out of the car and followed behind her, up the steps, and to the front door. Door number 47, to be exact. Angel knocked twice and waited. I stood behind her, looking like her bodyguard in my suit. I knew I looked the same way I felt. Out of place.

Door number 47 opened. A dark-skinned man, who looked to be in his mid-thirties, answered the door wearing a muscle shirt, and a pair of *True Religion* jeans. A gun was on his hip like it was a part of his wardrobe.

"Angel, what brings you here? Big Ken finally let you off the leash." The man laughed as he walked off, leaving the door opened, inviting us in. Angel walked in with my dumbass right behind her. I closed the door and locked it. I did it for my own safety. I was afraid someone would try to barge in and take what little money I had on me.

"Big Ken sent me to get the money you owe him," I heard Angel say as I walked in the room with them.

"Who the hell is this?" the man said, pointing at me like I wasn't the only other person in the room who was obviously out of place.

I opened my mouth to speak, but Angel beat me to it.

"He's the least of your worries. Now if you can grab what's owed then we can be out."

"Tell Big Ken I'm a little short. I know I owe him one-fifty, all I got is a hunnit. Tell him I'ma come through with the rest before he can miss it."

"Dip, when are you not short on your payments! What did Big Ken tell you the last time? Just because you're his cousin, that doesn't mean that you're exempt from the laws of the hustle. He told you the last time that that would be your last time coming up short. Didn't he?" Angel said.

I looked at Dip and hoped he had all of the money. I was ready to go. Dip stood up, and I took a step back. He lightly chuckled, seeing how nervous I was. Dip walked out the room. Seconds later, he came back with a black gym bag in his hand. He tossed the bag at Angel's feet.

"That's a hunnit. Tell him I'ma get the rest to him when I get it," Dip said as he sat back down.

Angel let out a menacing laugh. I swear she sounded like she had the devil in her when she did it. Angel reached in her purse and came out with a small gun. She aimed it at Dip. Dip smiled like something was actually funny about the whole situation. I turned and looked at the TV, wondering what the hell was he laughing at.

"Put that lil thang away before you hurt yo'self," Dip said with a smile on his face. I opened my mouth to speak. My mouth was dry like I had been eating cinnamon straight out the jar. Angel took a step closer to Dip, gun aimed at his head.

"Mr. Stevens," Angel said.

I wondered why she was calling my name at a time like this. I didn't get a chance to answer her as she said,

"Attorney-client privilege means that whatever you see or hear cannot be used against me in court, right? So, that means you cannot testify on anything I do or say, right?" I nodded from behind her. "Yes, but I have to be your lawyer before you do any kind of crime."

"How much would you charge to represent me then?" She asked, the gun still aimed at Dip.

"Depends on the case."

"A murder case," she said, causing Dip to laugh out loud.

"I'm expensive. My starting price would be at forty to fifty grand just to take your case. Almost a hundred grand to take it to trial!" I said, wondering where this was going.

"That bag by my feet. That's your payment!" she said as she let off two quick shots in Dip's face. He died with a smirk on his face.

The shots echoed throughout the small apartment. I stood in a daze as I watched blood seep from the two holes in his face. They were deep, permanent holes that an undertaker would have to know magic to fill. Angel faced me like nothin' had just happened. Like she didn't just kill a man right in front of me.

"Catch!" Angel said, tossing the murder weapon at me. Off instinct, I caught the gun. Once I realized what I had just done, I dropped it to the floor. Angel laughed as she took a scarf from her purse. She used the scarf to pick the gun up, then she placed it in her purse. I began to pace; my mind was in shock.

"What did you just do? You kill—you killed him!" I shouted as realization finally hit me.

Angel shook her head and said, "No, you killed him."

My left eyebrow raised like the wrestler, The Rock. "No, I did not. Wh-why would…" I was going crazy.

Angel picked up the gym bag and unzipped it. There was a collage of dead presidents inside. "If you don't want to go to prison for murder, you better come with me," she said as she headed for the door.

I looked at the smirking dead man and swiftly walked behind Angel. The door was already open. I walked out first. Angel grabbed the outside doorknob and used her shirt to pull it close. Angel walked normally to her Porsche. She opened her trunk and tossed the gym bag inside, then closed it shut. I looked around, wondering how many people saw us walk inside the apartment. And of the people that saw us, how many knew Angel? As soon as I heard the doors unlock, I jumped in the passenger seat and crouched down.

Angel laughed as she saw me doing the best I could to hide my face. She crunk the engine up and sped out the apartments. It seemed as if we whisked past street lights in a blur. The whole ride back to my office, I was quiet. In my mind I was putting together a solid alibi. I would sneak quick glances at Angel. She would be talking under her breath to herself. I guessed she was doing the exact same thing I was doing.

As soon as she pulled up to my place of business, I didn't let the car go in *park* before I jumped out and walked as fast as I could to my building. "Mr. Stevens, wait!" Angel shouted behind me.

I stopped and sighed as I slowly faced her. "What!" I shouted.

Angel popped her trunk. "Don't forget your payment," she said, smiling.

I shook my head and said, "I don't want anything to do with that blood money."

She grabbed the money from the trunk and tossed the bag at my feet. "You don't have any other option. Either you take the money, or end up just like Dip, your choice."

I stared at the little woman that spoke like a giant. She didn't look like she would hurt a fly, let alone kill someone. But looks can definitely deceive you. "Why are you doing this? I don't even know you. I never did anything to hurt you, or your husband. Just—" I huffed as I exploded. "You're a murderer! You killed that man in cold blood!" I shouted.

Angel shook her head and said, "No. *You* killed him in cold blood."

Now it was my turn to shake my head. "I saw you kill him. The murder weapon is in your purse." I pointed towards the car.

Angel laughed. "Yes, I killed him. Of course I did. You saw me, you were there. But, who else saw it? Dip? He's dead. And dead men don't testify. Look around, do you see all of those cameras? Those cameras show you leaving with me, and coming back with me. And let's not forget, the murder weapon has your prints on it. Or did you forget?"

I shook my head in disbelief. She had planned this. She set me up from the very beginning. "Why are you doing this to me? What do—" Then the thought came to me. "Is this your husband's doing? Did he put you up to this so that I could lower my price?"

"Fuck my husband!" She fumed.

Her sharp words caught me by surprise. "I-I thought you wanted me to help your husband stay free?" I said, confused.

"No. What I want is for you to get my husband as much time as you can possibly get him. As much as the system allows. If you do that, I'll pay you the money in this bag, another hundred grand, and I'll make that gun with your prints on it disappear. Believe me, I'm dead ass serious. If you try to play me, I'll turn that gun in, and tell the authorities that you forced me into it. Who do you think they'll believe? You or lil' ol' me?"

I shook my head. She wasn't no damn Angel. She was the devil in the flesh!

4

BIG KEN

The Next Day

I yawned and stretched as I rolled out of bed. I sat at the foot of the bed, looking around for my wife, Angel. She was nowhere in sight. Last night she came home in the wee hours of the night. We got into a big fight, as usual. Which resulted in me putting her in her place, I mean, me showing her whose fist was bigger and stronger. Me putting my hands on her always got her attention.

I remember years ago, when me and Angel were newlyweds. Nothing but happiness surrounded us. We traveled the world together, showing everyone what real love looked like. Couples were envious of us when we posted pictures on the gram or Facebook. There was nothing Angel wanted for. She had everything a wife could ever dream of.

My feet were deep in the drug game. I mean, I was up to my knees in it. My uncle, Turtle, was the sole supplier for the Triple D. Pallets of cocaine and heroin flowed through the city, and my uncle was the man to get it from. Turtle raised me in the streets. He showed me the rules of the game at an early age. People swore he was my father and not my uncle. Being that he raised me from the age of six until adulthood, I looked at him as a father figure.

My mother, Ronda—God rest her soul—she died in a heroin house with a needle sticking out of her arm. I didn't care for her none. My mom had a drug habit, and an abusive one too. She was addicted to drugs. And she was addicted to beating me when she didn't have any. I guess that's where I got my abusive skills from. My father, Damion, who was Uncle Turtle's blood brother, was incarcerated in the feds in Nevada for killing three federal agents that were working undercover to buy drugs from him. Did my father know if they were undercover agents?

I have no clue, and I never asked him. If he did know, I don't think the outcome would've been any different. He hated the police worse than he hated anythin' else.

I was adopted by my uncle at the age of six. From the day I was adopted by him, all I ever saw him do was make money. When it came to the streets, he was king. And the dope game was his castle. The top was his throne. He had lawyers, politicians, and the DPD in his pocket. Anything Turtle wanted, he got. Buildings, clubs, parks, whatever. Whatever he wanted, the mayor signed off on it. No one denied the king.

The streets loved and respected my uncle as if he was the president of the United States. Me being his only nephew, he gave me the only gift no one could ever take from me. The gift of knowledge. When it came to the game, I loved and respected it. I was groomed to one day fill the very large shoes of my uncle Turtle. The streets talked about my uncle as if there was no other subject to discuss. But the new trending topic came when he finally decided to step down from his throne, placing me in the chair he left vacant. Some people felt that I didn't deserve the keys to the city. Others feared the repercussions if they said it out loud. Me, on the other hand, I felt I deserved it. I knew I deserved it.

At the age of fifteen, I along with my day one nigga—Squirrel—started Bloody Money Bag. It started off as a neighborhood clique. We were just some north Dallas niggas that joined forces because everyone else was grouping up to try to take over our hood. See, majority of the other cliques were just petty hustlers, jack boys, or just plain ol' bums who grouped together to stunt.

Bloody Money Bag was the most envied, and respected. Our name spoke for itself. We had stupid gwap. It started with just me and Squirrel, and before long, we were twenty something deep. We didn't allow no bums. If you weren't already a go-getta, you weren't accepted. We all pulled our own weight. We didn't group up to roach off each other; we grouped up to build each other up. My uncle supplied me with dope, and I sold it to my clique at a fair price. Before you know it, Bloody Money Bag's name started ringing bells around Dallas and Fort Worth. Even though we were all teens in grade school, we had grown men trying to get down with us.

Years passed and Bloody Money Bag was still the clique to be reckoned with. I was still the head of Bloody Money Bag, and my day one guy—Squirrel—was still my right-hand man. Our numbers had grown from twenty to hundreds. Uncle Turtle was still king, and we were all unstoppable. I graduated high school for the sake of my uncle. That was his only wish for me. He said that it looked good on paper when I finally did take his spot. He says no one likes a dumb hustler. He said graduating high school was the one thing he regretted not doing as a kid. When I graduated, I was happy that I did too. Uncle Turtle gave me twenty ki's for a graduation gift. I set the city on fire that day.

Three years later, I met my wife, Angel. It was at a strip club in Houston. On sight I just knew I had to have her. She had this glow about herself that lit the whole club up. Seeing her, that was all it took for me to want to save her. And that's exactly what I did. Angel and I got married only a few months later. Well, almost a year later. But the day she moved into my house, I felt in my heart that she was my wife. Our wedding was the largest wedding Dallas had ever witnessed. Everything was just as I imagined it would be, perfect. Uncle Turtle stepped down the same day I got married. He told me that day that I had finally become a man. It was that day that he handed me all the keys he had, and his plug. It was like ever since I met Angel, I was on top of the world. Nothing could stop me. Nothing! Until.

Ten months ago, I got a call from one of my most lucrative custo's. He was in need of twenty ki's, and he needed them at that moment. I usually would send a worker to deliver the work, but I had twenty ki's in my duck-off spot that I had been meaning to move around. I insisted that Short Dan meet me at the washateria on Forest Lane and Audelia to pick up the work. It was a normal Friday. Well, at least I thought it was.

I sat in the washateria like I had dirty clothes in the washer. I didn't, though. But I did have some dirty money that I was anxious to get. As I sat there, Short Dan strolled in the washateria with a new look. He used to look confident, and upbeat. That day, he seemed off, timid, if I must say, even a little wary. Short Dan walked in with a Footlocker bag in his hand. He sat across from me at the picnic table.

"You got it with you?" Short Dan asked. I should've known something was up that day. He'd never done that in the past. Short Dan knew, whenever we ever met to do an exchange, we never asked or brought up drugs or money. He knew my end was always solid. And from our previous encounters, I thought his was too. Never having any funny feelings about him, I answered his question.

"What's my name? Don't I always handle my end?" I showed him my diamonds that covered every tooth I had. Short Dan didn't look at me long; he turned his head and grabbed the Footlocker bag from the floor. He sat the bag on the table in plain sight. Anger rose on my face as I snatched the bag down and sat it beside me.

"Look in the dryer, number twenty-three." I gave him dap and stood up. "Holla at me when you need me, you know I gotcha." He nodded and stared at me, then he dropped his head to his chest without saying a word. At that moment, I felt something was off. My eyes went to the front entrance, a group of plain-clothes agents rushed the front door with their guns drawn.

"Get on your knees, now!" One of them screamed at me. I looked at the nigga who I once respected for his word and hustle. He couldn't even look at me. He just took a step back as the agents slammed me to the ground.

I watched from a distance as another agent went to the dryer and snatched the bricks of cocaine from the dryer. The agent smiled as he held the dope up like he had just won a gold medal. I was cuffed and placed in the back of a cruiser. I was sent off to Mansfield Federal holdover. I hired a lawyer by the name of Emmanuel Stevens. I was referred to him by another cat that was locked up for somewhat similar charges. Emmanuel showed up within the next three hours wearing an expensive Tom Ford suit. I knew it was expensive because I had the same exact suit in my closet at home. He looked like money, which was a good sign. My million-dollar bond was posted on a PR lawyer bond. Emmanuel didn't tell me if he could keep me from going to prison or not, but he did say that if I gave him ninety-five large, he would damn sure try.

Sadly, the feds seized all of my assets, and placed a hold on all of my bank accounts. Anything that was in my name was snatched up and used as evidence against me. All I had left was the house that was in my uncle's name, my car, Angel's car, a plug that was still riding with me, and all the money the streets owed me.

Since the arrest, the feds have been all over me. With them watching my every move, I haven't been able to hustle like I used to. They have been keeping a car parked outside my house with a 24-hour surveillance. I've been beyond stressed out, wondering what the outcome would be once I go to trial. Since I haven't been able to hustle, I picked up a new habit. At first, I was an occasional drinker. I would have to be at an event or something to pop a bottle.

Now, I drink as soon as I wake up. It's all I want to do now. It's the only thing that eases the pain I've been feeling.

The bad side of my new habit is my temper and attitude. It's like the more I stay in the house, the angrier I am. Being in the house 24/7 made me hate my home. The only person that I have to keep me company is Angel. And lately, it's like all she ever does is nag. It got to the point where the more I drink, the more she nags. The only way to shut her up was to put my fist in her mouth.

On the other hand, my clique was still the deadliest in the streets. But I had seemed to have lost a lot of respect. Me being MIA from the streets gave niggas the ability to test me. They knew I was under the bird's eye, so they used that to their advantage. Niggas that owed me money went weeks at a time without paying me, and when they did, they were always short. My own blood cousin—Dip—even treated me like a peon. It was taking everything in me to not say *fuck the feds*, and go to the streets with my Glock out demanding everything that's owed to me. Niggas felt that they were getting away, and I wasn't feeling that.

I walked to the TV room and sat on the couch. I turned the TV on ESPN. Max was on TV talking about who he thought would win the Errol Spence versus Terrence Crawford fight. I was from the city, and I was a big fan of boxing, but I was going to stay away from betting on anyone. I was already in a lose-lose situation. I wasn't tryna take any more losses.

My cell started ringing on the table. I snatched it up and answered it. "Speak," I said into the phone.

"What you got goin', bruh?" My day one nigga Squirrel spoke into the phone.

"Shit, watching ESPN. What's the play?"

"I went by the grocery store to get the shit you had on the list. A lot of shit you had on the list, they didn't have. You told me to get a few bags of apples for the candy apples. I went to the Krogers on the south side—they were short like twenty!" Squirrel said in code.

I shook my head. He was saying how niggas was still coming up short on my bread. That was something I couldn't have. "Aye, come get me. It's long overdue."

5

ANGEL

I parked in front of Ken's spots in the north. I placed my Chanel frames over my eyes to hide my upgraded black eye. After I killed Dip, I convinced Emmanuel to go along with my plan. After I left Emmanuel's office, I went home and showered. I had a huge smile on my face as I let the water cascade down my body. All of a sudden, the shower curtain slung open. I stared at a drunken Ken. I already knew what time it was. Ass whooping time.

Ken questioned me about where I'd been all night, and why am I coming in his house at the wee hours of the morning. I came up with the best lie I could, but even that wasn't suffice enough. Ken's hand came across my face so hard and fast I didn't see it coming. My head slammed into the shower wall hard. There was blood all over. Luckily, I was already in the shower. I don't recall how long I was out, but I woke up in the shower, naked, and the water was still running.

I went to our bedroom and stared at Ken as he slept on his stomach in our bed. It took everything in me not to kill him in his sleep. I was sick and tired of being sick and tired. It seemed like the only time he wasn't slapping me around was when he was asleep. I had means to put him to sleep, for good. But truthfully, I think that's exactly what he wanted. He would rather die than to spend his every waking moment behind bars. Killing him in his sleep would be too easy. That's why I wanted him to suffer.

The next morning, I woke up before Ken did, as usual. Ken wanted me to make sure all the money in his stash spot was accounted for because it was time for him to re-up again. Never had he ever let me get close to his main stash, but with the feds being on his neck, he needed someone he could trust.

Ken's main spot was on Forest Lane and Audelia in an apartment complex called Ben Creek. Ben Creek produced a minimum of fifty grand a week in sales. It was the spot Ken had the longest.

I stepped out of my Porsche, the sun settling on my smooth skin. My sunglasses had become a permanent part of my wardrobe. The only time I felt comfortable taking them off was when I was at home. I knocked on the door to the trap. The door locks sounded, and I could hear a log being moved from the door frame. Bull stood on the other side of the door with a Glock 40 in his hand.

"Beautiful, you're here early this week, huh!" Bull said as he stepped aside to let me in. Bull was Big Ken's worker. He wasn't your normal nickel and dime hustler. No, Bull was a brick hustler. Big Ken placed Bull in one of his slow rolling spots just to put some money in Bull's pocket. Bull took the opportunity and ran with it. Bull turned the spot into one of Ken's best traps. Ken gave Bull a promotion, moving him from the spot in the Villa Vistas to the spot in Ben Creek.

I had known Bull since he was a young pup. He would always sneak into *Temptations* when I worked there. He was one of my faithful customers. The look on his face when Big Ken brought me around was priceless. I had never given Bull any pussy, so he didn't have anything he could tell Big Ken on me about. Every time Bull saw me, he would always say how Big Ken stole me from him, and how one day he would make it to Ken's level in the game and win me back. I would always laugh at Bull. Not that he was ugly, or anything like that. I just didn't date workers. I was a boss bitch, which meant I only fucked with boss niggas.

The sad thing was, I led Bull on to think that one day, if he ever made it to Ken's level in the game, maybe I would consider him. Bull started saving every dollar he made, putting it together to score weight from Ken, just to flip, and do it all over again. Bull didn't think I noticed, but I did. He was a true hustler, the best Ken had on his team. I knew if I ever wanted my plan to succeed, I would need Bull on my side. So, I did what any bad bitch of my caliber would do. I dangled my pussy on a string over his head like a boss bitch is supposed to. Niggas were soft behind pussy. It is the best weapon a woman has. The one thing God regretted making.

"Y'all know what's up. Step out until she gets done

taking care of business," Bull said to his three trainees. As they walked out the apartment, Bull locked the door behind them. I walked to the bedroom and went to the closet. I pulled out a pocket knife from my purse. I opened the blade and used it to pull off the caulk from the wall. The side wall swung open like a door. Inside the wall was another wall, only this one was made up of dead presidents.

"Bull, can you get me a duffle bag from under the bed!" I shouted. I looked over my shoulder to see Bull staring at my ass. I didn't make it no better being that my Chanel shorts were all up my ass. I shook my head at him. "Go!" I said, snapping him from his lustful trance.

Bull grabbed the bag from under the bed. He walked over to me with the bag held open. Each block of wrapped bills was counted out at twenty grand a block. I counted out forty blocks and stacked them up neatly inside the bag. As I bent over to zip the bag up, my glasses fell from my face. Bull snatched them up before I could.

I looked into his eyes. His mouth turned. I could see the anger written all over his face. His hand went to my cheek, right under my black eye. "Damn, ma. What the fuck happened to yo' eye?"

I grabbed my glasses and told a bold face lie. "I had a fight with this chick at the mall." The lie came out so quick, it sounded like the truth.

"That bitch must got a fist like a grown ass man," Bull said. I placed my glasses over my eyes. "You know, if you was my woman, you'll never have to worry about me putting my hands on you."

"Whatever!" I spat. "That's exactly what Ken said." As

soon as the words left my mouth, I wished I could take them back.

"Ken's a bitch! His time is up. The only reason you're still with him is because you're bonded by vows. But, when the feds carry him off, I'ma carry you off."

I looked into Bull's eyes. His words seemed genuine. Maybe it was his consistency, or the fact that I too felt that Ken's time was up. It was beyond up; his time was long overdue. "Bull, what would you say if I told you that I was planning on taking over Ken's entire operation?"

"Then I would have to ask you what took you so damn long." He laughed, bringing a smile to my face. "I would also tell you that you'll need a nigga like me on yo' team. A nigga that will kill for you, and die for you. Because if you plan on taking over Ken's operation, then you have to know that his enemies are yours as well."

"Enemies?" I said, not knowing he had any.

"Yeah," he laughed. "What? You thought the game only came with friends?"

"I know, but I thought—"

"You thought he didn't have any because he never let you see 'em."

"So, tell me who's his enemy?"

"Enemies." He corrected me. "The Block Boys," he said. I had heard of them, but they were from Waco Texas, and a few were scattered out around Dallas.

"Bishop and his crew. They've been after Ken since Turtle handed him the crown. Supposedly, Ken and Squirrel killed Bishop's brother a year ago in Fort Worth, at *Temptations.*

I tried to think back a year ago, but nothing came to

mind. "It was on the fourth of July," Bull said. "Ken had bumped into Knight, who's Bishop's brother. They ended up arguing until shit got out of hand. I was there that night. Shit was wild. The whole B.M.B was there, so in the beginning, Knight was waiting on us to come out. They ambushed us, but Ken ended up getting the drop on Knight. Ken smoked him right in front of er'body. Even though it was self-defense, Bishop wasn't tryna hear shit. He's been dead on avenging his brother's death ever since."

I remembered now that he recapped the story. That night, when everything happened, Ken came home in a panic, destroying the clothes he had on, sweating like crazy. "So, you think Bishop will try to come at me?" I asked.

"Why not! You're Ken's wife, and you'll be the head of B.M.B.," he said. "But, we'll be ready for them when they do come after you, I can promise you that."

I nodded and played along. "So, if I make you my right hand, what will you want in return? I know nothing in life is free."

"Your respect, that's it," he said. I knew it was a bunch of BS. I couldn't do nothing but hold my laugh in. Niggas thought that because they were blessed with two heads, that they were smarter than women.

"So, where would you start, if you were in my shoes?" I asked.

"First things first, you'll have to take out what means the most to Ken. That way, once he's in the can, he won't have any soldiers that can interfere. Take out everyone that means anything to him. That way, he'll only have you to rely on. As long as he only has you, he'll have to trust you with everything. And I mean, everything."

I nodded as I pretended that he'd just told me something that I didn't know. What Bull didn't know was that I was already ten steps ahead of him and Big Ken.

"Who means the most to Ken, I mean besides me?" I asked.

"His uncle, Turtle!"

6

JANICE

Knock! Knock! Knock!

I used my knuckles to bang on the front door. I looked down at my phone and redialed Emmanuel's number. Two days in a row I went to work, and he was a no-show. That was so unlike him. When it came to his profession, he never missed work without informing me first.

I've been a part of Stevens' law firm for over three years now. I started off as an intern, filling in for his secretary, Malina. Malina had taken a trip to Paris, and somehow struck gold, catching the eye of a multi-million-dollar designer. Now Malina's a runway model for Chanel. Emmanuel ended up hiring me permanently, but not by default. I paved my way by making sure whatever he needed, I provided, even before he knew he needed it. I was always very attentive to him and his needs.

Emmanuel, who actually likes to be called Manny for short, always treated me with nothing but respect. I will admit, I would sometimes dress provocatively, hoping he'll notice me. Manny was a helluva catch. He was every bit of the man of my dreams. Tall, dark, and very handsome. He was like a big cup of Starbucks coffee. I loved everything about him. Except, he was married.

Knock! Knock! Knock!

I banged on the door, again. Emmanuel's car was in his driveway, so I was sure he was at home. *Woof! Woof!* A dog barked inside the house. I placed my ear to the door. The lock sounded, forcing me to stand up straight. I fixed my hair, just in case his wife, Hannah, opened the door. The door swung open. Manny stared at me with a bottle of Jack in his hand. The bottle was almost empty. A pug dog stood guard, but behind him. Manny's hair was disheveled. His pants were hanging off of his butt. He stood before me shirtless; his chest hair seemed to have filled his middle torso completely.

"Janice, wha-what are you doing? I mean, what are you doing . . . here?" His words came out as a slur.

"I came by to make sure you were okay. You haven't come by the office in two days," I looked at him wondering what the hell was going on. I had never seen him in such a way.

Manny didn't respond; he just walked back to where he'd come from, leaving the door wide open. I took that as my invitation to come inside, so I did, closing the door behind myself. As I walked into the living room, I noticed how nice his house actually was. Everything seemed perfect, except for all the clothes that were thrown around, and the broken glass, with the half torn pictures.

Manny sat on the couch. His leg was propped up on his coffee table. "What happened to you? You look like someone you love dearly has passed away." *Or your wife left*, I thought to myself.

"Hannah," he said, then sighed. "She left . . . me." He sounded as if he wanted to cry, but his pride wouldn't let him.

My mouth dropped open. I had always heard that there was life and death in the tongue, but it had to be in the mind too. "You two just celebrated your anniversary," I said, still surprised.

Manny smiled as he brought the bottle of Jack to his lips. He took a swig then let the bottle rest on his stomach. "So much for celebrating, huh."

I shook my head. "Care to talk about it?" I was hoping he did. I needed some juicy drama in my life.

"I-I caught her cheating," he said with no emotion.

"How? Through a text or the internet?"

He shook his head and said, "I came home to celebrate our anniversary, and she was already celebrating. She was fucking my college roommate in our shower." He shook his head as if he was trying to get the images from his head.

"That's the least of my worries though," he said as he brought the bottle to his lips.

"Your wife having sex with your best friend can't be the least of your worries."

He looked at me as if he had a closet full of skeletons that I knew nothing about. "I'm a murderer," he said as he took another swig from the bottle. I snatched the bottle from his hand and dared him to try and get it back.

"A what?" I spat.

He laughed. "Well, at least until I can prove my innocence."

"Manny, what did you do? Did you kill your wife and best friend?" I asked as I looked around the room for blood.

"In my mind I did, but no, sadly they're still breathing." He took his feet from the coffee table and said, "You remember Kendrick Watson?"

I thought quickly and nodded. "Our current case, yes, I remember him."

He nodded and said, "Well, his loving wife paid me a visit two days ago. She came by to give me the payment for Mr. Watson." He shook his head in disgust, then he looked at me sideways. "You're probably just like them both!" he spat.

I went into defense mode. "Like, who?"

"Hannah and that evil bitch, Angel!"

I looked at him with wide eyes, wondering who was this Angel he was comparing me to. "I'm nothing like your cheating ass wife!" Manny looked at me stunned. He had never heard me use profanity, ever, and I didn't give a damn if he heard me use it for the first time. One thing I wasn't was a cheating ass woman.

"What about Angel, huh? You're going to kill someone and toss the gun at me to get my prints on it so you can blame the murder on me, huh!"

My mouth opened in shock. "Wait, what?" I was hoping I heard wrong, and that he was just drunk, talking out the side of his neck.

"You heard me right. I was tricked, bamboozled by another woman into trusting her, and I got the bad end of the stick, again. I guess it's true, bad guys do finish last."

I placed my hand on his knee. "Manny, stop, please! If

this is true, then you need to tell me what happened, everything."

Manny huffed, then said. "I fucked up, bad." Tears began to fall from his eyes. I began to think the worst. My mind was wondering if he had really killed someone.

"Manny, tell me everything, please!"

He placed his face in his hands then shook his head side to side. "She killed him, and then she tossed the gun at me. Off instinct, I caught it. My prints were all over the murder weapon. She has it, and she's holding it over my head."

"Who? And . . . and why would she do something like that?"

He looked up with red eyes and said, "Because I'm defending her husband."

I was beyond confused. "So, what does you defending her husband have to do with anything?"

"She wants me to throw the case, so he'll go to prison for the rest of his natural life."

I shook my head. Now I understood why he was drinking himself under the table. He was caught up in some *Lifetime* movie network shit. "So, what are you going to do?"

Manny loved his job. He was a good lawyer. No, good was an understatement. He was a great lawyer, one of the best there was. He took pride in his win percentage. I just knew he would do the right thing. I could bet my last dollar he would.

Manny looked at me. I smiled, hoping my smile could be the light at the end of his tunnel he was venturing through. "I'm going to do what she asked. I'm going to throw the case."

7

EMMANUEL

The Next Dat

Janice got me out of my funk as best as she could. She actually spent the entire night with me just to make sure I didn't drink anymore. I woke up with everything heavy on my mind. I know what I said to Janice yesterday, but I don't honestly think I can go through with it. Janice brought up the possibility of calling the cops, and explaining to them what really happened. I instantly declined that option. Angel had planned everything out thoroughly. Calling the cops would be as if I walked in the jail begging them to give me a life sentence for something I know I didn't do.

After I sobered up a little, Janice told me how she wasn't anything like my skank ass wife, or Angel. It was hard to believe anything she said because Hannah and Angel had ruined my ability to trust. Then Janice started professing her loyalty, telling me how she would go to bat for me, and be by my side through all of this, no matter the outcome. That was all it took for me to give in to her. That's how special women were. If it was one thing I learned since becoming an attorney, you feel like you can win any battle with the right support system behind you.

Now we were at my office. I had a meeting with the notorious Kendrick Watson to discuss his case. I was praying he wasn't bringing his conniving ass wife; I wouldn't be able to control myself around her presence.

"Mr. Watson, it's nice to see you smiling." I greeted Kendrick as we shook hands. "This is my secretary, Janice." Kendrick nodded and smiled at her.

"I'm doing okay, considering the possibility of my future," Kendrick said.

I nodded. "I understand. Trust me, if I was in your shoes, God forbid. But, I would be nervous too. But, like Allstate, you're in good hands. When it comes to cases like yours, dealing with them for so long, I have a knack for finding even the slightest mistake in a case that could either get you the shortest time possible, or no time at all."

"That's good to hear," Kendrick said, smiling.

"So, if you'll just follow me into my office, we can get started." I led the way with Kendrick behind me. I sat behind my desk as Kendrick sat across from me. He sat in the exact same chair his conniving ass wife sat in when she bamboozled me into going with her to get some money I knew I had no business getting.

"Kendrick, with the federal court system, they really do their homework before they come after you, or convict you." Kendrick nodded. "So, when they come after you, they basically have everything they need to lock you up for as long as they desire. See, since we both know this, it makes my job that much easier," I said as I typed on my computer.

"They'll have the drugs that they found in the public washer and dryer, as well as the marked bills, also a wire recording with your voice on it. Therefore, we can't pretend that the drugs were planted. You receiving that much money makes it look like a drug deal."

Kendrick nodded again, resting his chin on his fist. "So, what can we do?" he asked.

"We can do one or two things. One, we can go through with this trial, hope that the snitch and the arresting officers will slip up on the stand."

"What's the other option?" he asked.

"You can cop a plea deal."

Kendrick rubbed his hand through his waves. I could tell this case had stressed him out. The chances of spending the rest of your life in a cement box will break the strongest man. "In reality, you're looking at some prison time. What my goal is, is to get you the minimum."

"Like what?" he asked.

"Ten years at the least. Five, if I can persuade them that you're not a troublemaker. Seeing that you don't have any priors, convincing them won't be too hard to do."

"Ten years, damn! I guess that's not so bad."

"It's actually not. You'll do eighty-five percent, that's eight-and-a-half years. A blessing, if you ask me!" I said convincingly.

He nodded and said, "That sounds like a decent plan. Tell me what I need to do."

I wanted to say, *kill your wife and clear my name*. But,

instead I said, "Stay out of trouble, and far away from drugs, or anyone who's affiliated with drugs. Kendrick, I'm not new to this stuff. I may not be in the streets like you, but I've represented a lot of street cats just like you. I know when you make a lot of money selling drugs, you seem to get stuck in the game. It gets hard to walk away sometimes. But, for the sake of your freedom, you should at least consider it."

Kendrick nodded. "I'm already a step ahead of you on that. My hands are clear of all dealings. All I want is to get this bid over with, so that I can come back home." I nodded.

"I will do everything in my power to get you exactly what you want." I stood up and so did Kendrick.

We shook hands, then I walked him to the door. Kendrick turned to me and said, "If you need me, you can call my wife, Angel. She's been very supportive, and she'll make sure the message gets to me."

I sighed and nodded. I felt bad for him. He was naive, just like I was. He was like me, thinking that his wife was loyal and supportive. We were both blinded by love. He could learn like I did. Love isn't always what people make it out to be. Love isn't always cookies and cream. Love can be violent!

8

BIG KEN

After I left my attorney's office, me and Squirrel took a ride to pick up some money my bad business ass cousin Dip owed me. I had been hitting his line up all day. He did what he always did when he owed me some bread, let my call go straight to voicemail.

"What yo' lawyer talkin' 'bout?" Squirrel asked as he drove us through the Stiff Cliff.

I laughed and said, "Basically he said a nigga 'bout to go do some time. He said he will do his best to make sure I don't get a lot of time though. He told me to make sure I keep my hands clean, and to stay out of the spotlight."

Squirrel nodded and said, "So, what are you goin' to do?"

"I'ma take his advice and get out of the game."

Squirrel's gold grill peeked from behind his upper lip. "So have you figured out what you're going to do with the plug?"

I was hoping that this conversation never came up. All

my life, Squirrel has been my right-hand man. One would think he earned the right to take over my spot once I got out of the game. Don't get me wrong. He's never done anything wrong, and he's never given me a reason to not hand him the plug. When my attorney told me that he could get me the minimum of five years, I put together a plan. I guess you can call it a master plan. I had once told Angel that if a woman was ever in position to run a drug operation, she'll always succeed. Women took their jobs seriously, more serious than men. I planted a seed in Angel's mind, and I watered it by feeding her game, teaching her how to weigh, bag, and sell dope. She was the female version of me. When the feds got all over my trial, I had Angel take over the main operation. She would pick up the money, and drop off the packs. When I came up with the idea for Angel to take over, I really didn't consider Squirrel would be upset. I figured he would be a little disappointed, but he was my guy. I knew he would understand. I didn't know how I would break the news to him. I figured I'll cross the bridge when we got to it.

In response to the question Squirrel asked, I said, "You already know what's going on." Squirrel smiled, thinking that me saying that meant I was going to bless him with the plug. He nodded with a smile as he parked in front of Dip's spot.

"So, what's the deal with Dip? How we handling the situation?" Squirrel asked.

"If bruh ain't got my bread, I'ma send him to the creator, early. Family or not, I need every penny he owes me."

Squirrel nodded as we stepped out of the truck. I

nodded at a few cats as we walked past them up the stairs to Dip's spot. Squirrel stood behind me as I looked around. I knocked on the door and stared at it waiting for Dip to answer. I looked back to the parking lot, looking around for Dip's Monte Carlo. Once I spotted it, I shook my head in anger and banged on the door. Something told me to try the knob, so I did. The door opened. I looked back at Squirrel.

"Dip, it's yo' cousin, Ken!" I shouted. I didn't want the nigga to come out of nowhere shooting, thinking I was there to rob him.

Once I stepped foot in the living room, I knew where the foul odor came from. Death had a certain kind of smell. A smell once you smell it, you'll never forget it again.

"Damn, somebody got to him first, huh!" Squirrel said as he covered his nose with his hand. I stared at Dip as he looked off to a place only the dead could see. He had this funny looking grin on his face, like whoever killed him caught him in the act of smiling. I shook my head. I didn't know if I should be pissed off that someone killed my cousin, or upset that I didn't get a chance to do it myself. Don't get me wrong. I loved my cousin; he was family. We shared the same blood, but we didn't share the same principles. I never put myself into debt, and I always took care of my business.

"Come on, let's go. Whoever off'd this nigga most likely already got everything he had. Ain't no point in sticking around."

"What you gon' do about fam'?" Squirrel asked as he followed behind me.

"Catch him at heaven's gate and beat his bitch ass fo' dying with my bread."

9

BIG KEN

"How do I look?" Angel asked as she stood in front of the floor-to-ceiling mirror.

Angel looked amazing. Her box-styled braids were freshly done. No make-up, only lip gloss. She wore a red Fendi bodysuit that hugged her curves to perfection. Her heels were my favorite; they were red and silver with spikes on the toe. Her eyebrows were arched to a point, she looked as if she was about to go to a photo shoot instead of going to meet the plug, Luis.

"You look like you're trying to get Luis to take you from me," I joked.

Angel pushed me playfully and said, "Boy, please." She laughed. "I have to be the reflection of my man, right."

I smiled at her truth. Every time I went to see Luis, I always dressed to impress. Today was no different. Today I rocked a white and black Chanel cardigan with a white Chanel V-neck under it, a pair of all-white Chanel Khaki's with my all-white Chanel loafers.

"When I take you to see Luis, we have to look like we have everything under control, like we are the bag instead of still tryna get the bag," I said.

Angel kissed my cheek, a little lip gloss was still on my cheek as she pulled her lips away. "Not just my bag, but a Bloody Money Bag," she said with a smile on her face as she walked away.

Her ass swished in front of me as she walked. I couldn't help but smack her juicy ass, making it jiggle from my touch. "Don't start, we'll be late," she said, biting her lip. I laughed as we hopped in my Audi and bent the corner. "Damn, bae, how long are they going to stay here? Can't we do something about it?" Angel asked as we drove past the federal stalkers.

"Naw'l, babe, we can't do shit about it. The feds is the government, and the government do what the fuck they want."

Angel shook her head as she changed the radio station. "Put our shit on," I said as I hopped on the freeway. I pressed down on the gas pedal so everyone could end up in my rearview mirror. If the feds were still following us, I was sure I lost them by now. Angel pulled her gun from her purse and checked the clip. I laughed as Money Bag Yo began to rap.

'*When I look in the mirror what do I see / a reflection of me / when I'm in my ride and I look to the side / a reflection of me.*'

I bobbed my head to the music. I looked through the side mirror at my wife. She was in fact the true reflection of me. She was a gangsta, just like me. The past few days that I haven't been drinking reminded me of what me and Angel really had. The bond, the love we shared. I missed her. I missed us.

I turned the radio down from the steering wheel. Angel looked at me like I was crazy. "Why'd you do that? That was my favorite part." She went to turn the radio back up but I popped her on the hand, stopping her.

"I want to talk to you about something," I said as she folded her arms and poked her lips out like a kid.

"Nope, I'm mad." She pouted.

I couldn't do nothing but laugh. She was spoiled rotten. "You lil mad, or you big mad?" I teased.

She faced the passenger side window and said, "I'm big mad!"

I shook my head, laughing. "Angel, fo'real."

She faced me smiling. "What's on your mind, daddy?"

"Us."

"What about us?" she asked.

"I-I-uhm. I want you to know that I'm sorry for the way that I've been treating you. For ignoring you, and for putting my hands on you." I shouldn't have put my hands on you, or took my anger out on you."

Angel looked at me surprised. It was the very first time I apologized for hitting her. All the other times I put my hands on her, I never apologized. I would just buy her some flowers, or some new jewelry, or even a new car as my way of saying I was sorry. But seeing how she's been picking up my slack, delivering money to my lawyer, dropping off work to the home team, I realized that she's been down for me in ways that I never imagined. When I told her how I found my cousin dead, she offered to put ten stacks on the head of whoever did it. She was my rider.

The car was quiet. I looked over to my wife, she was in tears.

———

Angel

THIS NO-GOOD, dirty-dick, bitch-ass nigga! He has the nerve to finally apologize to me. This no-good slick-dick ass nigga has beat me over twenty times, and he thinks one fuckin' apology will make me forget it and it'll all go away. Hell . . . the fuck . . . nawl!

So why was I crying? I don't fucking know! Maybe because I've been waiting for him to apologize for months now. But, his apology was too late. Maybe five months ago he would've had me, but certainly not now. I was already tired of being sick and tired. He could shove his sorry right up his black ass!

"Angel, I'm sorry. Don't cry." He tried to console me.

I wiped my tears with the side of my finger. Ken saying he was sorry made me hate him even more. "I know I should've since said I was sorry, Angel. But I'm saying it now. Angel, I'm really sorry."

'*You think!*' I thought to myself.

We pulled up to a beautiful suburban area with massive mansions. The area was a gated community, but we made it through by tailing another car. "You're not going to say anything?" Ken asked me. I looked out the window, amazed. Our home was huge, but theirs was massive.

I finally sighed and said, "Let's just take care of this and we can talk about it later." I had business on my mind.

He couldn't blame me; I learned it from him. Business over bullshit.

Ken didn't say anything as we pulled up to Luis' estate. As we stopped in front of his main gate, Ken leaned out the window and pressed the gate button. A woman's voice came over the speaker.

"Yes," the soft voice said.

"It's Kendrick Watson, for Luis!" Ken said with his head out the window like he was at a fast food drive thru. The gate buzzed open. The large iron gates opened and Ken drove up the long driveway. It seemed like the closer we got to the house, the larger it appeared. I looked around the large property. There were armed guards surrounding the property as they overlooked the gardeners while they worked. Security cameras were all over the property watching our every move.

Ken looked at me and said, "Luis is on a whole 'nother level."

"I see," was all I said as we pulled up to the front of the house. As soon as we parked, two Hispanic men met us at the front door. Ken popped the trunk as we stepped out of the car. My red bottoms clicked on the pavement as I walked around the trunk. Ken lifted the trunk as I hung my purse strap over my shoulder.

"When we get inside, let me do the talking," Ken mumbled as he grabbed the two duffle bags full of money. I closed the trunk and followed behind him.

"Filipe, Jorge!" Ken greeted the two guards as he handed them the duffle bags.

"Ken, good to see you, Hombre. Luis is waiting for you by the pool!" one of the men said.

We walked through the house with Filipe and Jorge right behind us. I looked at the house, marveled. It was even bigger on the inside. The staircase was made out of glass that curved all the way to the fourth floor. There was a gold-plated elevator by the stairs that just blew my mind. Even though I was mad at Ken, the excitement took me over the edge as I touched his shoulder and pointed to the gold elevator.

"Babe, he got a fuckin' elevator in his house. And it's made of gold!" I said excitedly.

"You should see his house in Honduras, it's twice this size," Ken said as I shook my head in awe. It was amazing the shit money could buy.

As we made it to the large pool, Luis stood up to greet us. "Kendrick, how are you, Mijo?" Luis asked as he hugged Ken like he was his own son.

I smiled as I stood to the side of Kendrick. "I'm good, Luis," Ken said as he looked back at me with a smile on his face. "This is my wife, Angel. Angel, this is Luis."

Luis held his arms open and said, "She's beautiful, Kendrick. What is a guy like you doing with a woman as beautiful as this?" Luis teased as he looked back at me with a smile on his face.

Luis was a short, gray-haired Hispanic. His skin was the color of bronze. For a second I thought he could be mixed with black. He held a huge smile, a smile of respect as he looked at Ken. His smile wasn't fooling me though. I knew his old ass was a straight killer.

"I told Angel on the way over that you were going to try and take her from me," Ken joked.

Luis laughed. "I couldn't keep up with her. She looks like she's a handful."

"Ken laughed and said, "Two handfuls." Luis sat down and offered us a seat.

"I hope you two are hungry. Isabella cooked her famous enchiladas."

I smiled and nodded as Ken said, "I'm starving."

I looked at the large pool. The water was blue, like it had been imported from the Bahamas.

A maid pushed a metal cart to our table and placed a hot plate in front of us, then another in front of an empty seat. "My daughter, Lluvia will be down in just a second," Luis said.

Ken looked up from his plate in shock. "Lluvia is here? When did she get back?"

"A week ago. She got tired of staying at the mansion in Honduras, so she decided to come back," Luis explained.

I looked at Ken, wondering who Lluvia was, and why did he look the way he did when he found out she was back in the States. Then I got my answer. A Hispanic woman walked out the back door in our direction. She was drop-dead gorgeous. I mean, she wasn't sexier than me, but I do give props where props are due. I'm not a hater.

Lluvia strutted over to our table with a pink Gucci swimsuit on. She wore a pink see-through linen Gucci robe over her bathing suit. And Oh . . . My . . . Gawd! The bitch had on a badass pair of wood bottom Manolo's on that made me gush in jealousy. She had long, curly jet-black hair. Her hair bounced with each step she took. She had to be my height, maybe shorter. Her cheeks were full; her body was tight and lean. She even had a navel piercing that made her six-packs stick out.

As Lluvia got close to the table, she gasped once she noticed Ken. "Oh my God! Ken-Ken!" Lluvia damn near screamed as she covered her mouth as if she was seeing her favorite celebrity for the first time.

Ken-Ken! I know this bitch didn't! Ken stood up and had the nerve to hug her. A little too long for my taste. As they pulled apart, Lluvia eyed Ken up and down. "Ken-Ken, you look amazing!" she said,

Ken blushed like a fuckin' girl and said, "Thank you. And you look—" I cleared my throat for all of mankind to hear. Ken looked at me and said, "Oh, Rain, this is my wife, Angel."

Lluvia looked at me, surprised. "I didn't know you had got married. Tha-that's . . . sweet," she said as she took her seat beside Ken.

I was glad she wasn't sitting beside me, 'cause I had means to kick her skank taco-eating ass under the table. "Rain? I thought your name was Lluvia?" I said, looking at Ken.

Lluvia picked up her glass of water and said, "It's pronounced, U-via, but in Spanish my name means, *Rain*. Back in the day when me and Ken-Ken were dating, he could never really pronounce my name so he would always just call me Rain," Lluvia said as she smiled at Ken.

"Oh, you two dated?" I asked, surprised.

Ken picked up his glass of water and buried his face in it. He had somehow forgot to inform me that he once dated the plug's daughter.

Ken cleared his throat and said, "Yeah, we dated a little

over five years ago, right before Uncle Turtle got out the game. Before I met you." He made sure to throw that part in.

Lluvia laughed and said, "Right after I had a miscarriage, we decided to go our separate ways. Losing our son, Kelvin, was hard for the both of us. I was six months pregnant when it happened."

The more this bitch kept talking, the worst it got for Ken. First, he didn't tell me that he once dated the plug's daughter. Then he made sure not to tell me that he had got her pregnant. What else did he so-called forget to mention to me?

Ken sat quietly. He knew his ass was going up shit's creek without a paddle. Luis noticed the look on my face as I crossed my arms. "So, Ken," Luis said, changing the subject, "how's your fed case looking?" Just then, Isabella came over and placed hot plates in front of us. The food smelled amazing, my stomach growling instantly.

"Honestly," Ken sighed. "I will be going away for a little while. Which is understandable. When a man does a crime in the league we're in, we have to consider that one day they will catch us, and when they do, we have to man up and pay our dues. Me, I'm content with that. It comes with the game, and I know what I signed up for."

Luis nodded. "Whenever you come home, I'll make sure you come home in style. And if you ever want to continue your profession, I'll make sure you have everything you need."

"That's exactly why I'm here. I know I'm going to prison. Like I said, I'm content with that. But I still have a huge family to feed. I don't want to leave them with nothing, feel me? I would rather put someone in my spot, at least until I come home."

"Who do you have in mind? Your right-hand man, Squirrel?" Luis asked.

Ken shook his head. "No."

"Then who?" Luis asked.

Ken looked at me and said, "My wife, Angel."

————

Ken

WHEN I SAID Angel's name, Luis looked at me like I was insane. I knew what he was thinking. This is a man's game. The only thing the women were good for in this game was cooking, cleaning, and taking care of the kids. That's how Luis knew the game to be. But Luis didn't know my bitch —Angel.

"Kendrick, I look at you like your family. Like you're my own son. You and I both know the game we're in. It's deadly and violent. This isn't braiding hair or doing nails. This is a billion-dollar business."

I nodded. I had thought about all of that. "I understand, Luis. But I once recall you once said that if you retire, you would turn the business over to Rain," I reminded him.

"Yes, but that was before—" Luis stopped mid-sentence. Rain looked at him. She had no idea she was going to be the head of the whole operation.

Luis had planned to hand the cartel over to Lluvia. She wasn't as deadly as Luis, but mentally she could run the entire operation in her sleep. The Villano Cartel was Rain's, until enemies of Luis came at him hard, at his only child, Lluvia. At the time, Lluvia was pregnant with our son. Luis' enemies kidnapped her and beat her for months until we finally found her. By that time, she had lost so much weight she was unrecognizable. She was right at nine months pregnant when we found her, and she had suffered a painful miscarriage.

"Luis, you told me once before that if I ever needed anything, and you did say anything. To just ask. So, I'm asking that you just trust me on this."

Luis thought for a second. He had always been a man of his word. He took his word seriously; it was all a real man had. Luis huffed and said, "Okay, I'll do it. But, I can't afford to front her the way I do you. Money up front, then she'll get the product. I'm only doing this for you because I'm a man of my word." Luis looked at Angel and said, "Angel, don't take what I said personally, it's nothing against you."

Angel smiled and said, "I understand, Ken always taught me, business is never personal"

Luis nodded and cracked a smile. "She's the reflection of me," I said, smiling.

Lluvia let the air out of her lungs like a flat tire. I had to end this meeting, and fast. I knew Angel; she wouldn't be able to stand under Lluvia for too much longer.

"So, when do you want to do the first exchange, Angel?" Luis asked her.

"As soon as possible, tomorrow, if you can make it happen," Angel said, sounding like a true boss bitch.

"I'm ready now," Luis said. "I'm going to keep the prices the same as I was with Kendrick. Thirteen per ki of snow, fifteen per ki of girl. Everything with my stamp on it will be the best quality. I'll make sure the dope gets to you once the money gets to me."

Angel nodded and said, "That's fair."

"Do you have a number in mind? Something you'll want to start off with? I advise you to start off with something small," Luis said.

"Yes. I have a number in mind!" Angel said with a serious face.

Luis nodded. "Let me hear it."

"A hundred ki's."

10

BULL

I knew sooner or later Angel would have me caught up in her bullshit. It was only a matter of time, and now the time had come. When I told Angel that she would need to kill Turtle, I didn't think that she would ask me to do it, but I always had it in the back of my mind, if she ever asked me to do anything, I would do it. How could I tell her no when she promised me a nice bag to do it. I asked her what if I was killed in the process? I was shocked when she said, "Then you died for a good cause."

I've heard rumors of how evil Angel really was. How people see her pretty smile and fall for her charms. Not really knowing she's the devil's advocate. That she's the worst angel of God's creation, a fallen angel. The angel that used to be good, that used to be pure, but she turned mad, possessed, and evil. I was just glad that I was on her good side. I knew once I showed her my loyalty, she would eventually let me take the seat that Big Ken left vacant.

When we were at Ken's trap, I wanted to kiss her so

damn bad, but I just didn't want to seem thirsty. I can't lie, some niggas just plain stupid. Ken had a bag bitch, one that's down for him no matter what. She would kill for him, even steal for him. She's a go-getta, one of a kind. And what does Ken go and do—slaps her around. He turns a loyal bitch into the worst kind of woman. One that's fed up.

I sat in my Camaro behind the three percent tint. I was in Collin County, parked outside of Bent Tree golf course. I had followed Turtle's Yukon here. I was just going to hop out in broad daylight and clap him, but his security was on point. There were four of them, street niggas in suits that I had watched in the game growing up. I couldn't help but look at them and laugh. They were dressed in black suits like they were the C.I.A, like they were protecting the president. But Turtle was a made man; he was well worth armed guards.

As I sat in my car, I started getting impatient waiting for them to come out of the country club. The nigga has been playing golf for over three fuckin' hours. I mean, how exciting could it be swatting a ball into a small hole? When street niggas start making major paper, they start acting bougie. Like they too good to go to the hood and play basketball. Instead, they'll go play golf with some politicians that only deal with them because they got money.

I laughed and shook my head. "I will never change up!" I said out loud to myself.

Fuck, where this nigga at? I thought to myself. I looked up and noticed Turtle's so-called security team leading him to his Yukon. I cranked my Camaro up and waited. Turtle shook hands with a short Caucasian male, then they parted ways.

I didn't know how I was going to do it, but I was going to get the job done. One ki was a lot for a young nigga my age. But twenty ki's, that was life-changing for me. I'd cross my mama for twenty ki's.

The Yukon with Turtle in it pulled off. As they exited the parking lot, I pulled out behind them. Not too close to where they could notice me, but close enough to where I wouldn't lose them. The plan was simple. I was going to wait until he got close to his house, pull up beside his truck and Swiss-cheese him and his goons with my AK. I'm talking 'bout execution style. I just had to make sure no one was around to see anything.

The closer we got to his house, the more nervous I became. I wasn't nervous because I was afraid to kill his old ass. Fuck no, I was a killa at heart. I was nervous because I didn't want to fuck this shit up. This was an opportunity of a lifetime, and I only had one shot to get this right. One mistake, and I was dead.

The Yukon turned on Turtle's street. I placed the AK across my lap and let the window down. I sped up to get a little closer to them. As soon as the Yukon was to stop, I planned on giving them the whole fuckin' clip.

The Yukon stopped at a stop sign. I got ready to make my move. I looked through my rearview mirror and noticed a white van speeding behind me. I'm talkin' 'bout the van was doing damn near a hundred. As I looked back in front of me, the Yukon was pulling off. As I put my foot on the gas, the white van sped past me, swerved, and then stopped right in front of the Yukon.

The Yukon's brakes smashed. The slide door to the van opened, and four masked men hopped out with their guns blazing. The shit happened so fast, it didn't register in my mind what was going on until I saw one of the gunmen open the backdoor to the Yukon. One of Turtle's dead bodyguards' body fell from the truck to the pavement. Turtle stepped out of the Yukon with his hands raised high above his head as a gunman shoved him into the back of the van.

I boldly drove past the driver's side of the van. I looked the driver directly in his eyes. I wasn't sure if the driver knew who I was, but I damn sure knew who he was. I knew Bishop's face anywhere.

Angel

"I'M PROUD OF YOU, BABE," Ken said as we walked in the house. "The way you handled business in front of Luis, that's how a boss bitch does it, fo'real, babe." Ken applauded me.

I ignored the shit out of him. How the fuck is he going to congratulate me for being me! The fuck! He must've thought I magically forgot about his babymama, Lluvia. Oh, my bad, Rain! Let's not forget his unborn seed, Kelvin. Kelvin! What kind of name is that anyway? Considering that Lluvia's Hispanic, I would've thought that the baby would have a Hispanic name or something close to one. Certainly not Kelvin. That's probably why the baby died. He didn't want to enter the world as Kelvin. Lord forgive me!

I walked into our bedroom and kicked off my heels.

Ken walked in the room behind me. He was still talking out the side of his neck about how well I did at Luis' house. Ken wasn't even paying attention as I took my jewelry off and tied my hair into a tight ponytail.

Even though I was tired of Ken putting his hands on me, tonight we were about to throw down. But I had a trick up my sleeve for his ass tonight. It's a little something I like to call, the element of surprise.

Ken walked in the adjoining bathroom. I waited for the right moment. I reared back as far as my arm would allow and clocked him in the jaw as he was peeing. I hit him so hard that he started peeing all over the bathroom floor and walls. He was in a daze.

"Bitch, what the—" Ken shouted as I ran out the bathroom.

I wasn't afraid of him anymore. The only reason I ran was so that I could get to some open space. As the old saying goes, 'Space and opportunity'. In the bathroom Ken would've beat my ass all over the sink and toilet, hell, the tub too. I had to give myself a fighting chance, even if it was a slim one.

"I got yo' bitch, bitch!" I said as I punched my open palm out of anger. I was ready and heated.

Ken stumbled out of the bathroom clutching his jaw. I held my fist open, ready for the fight of my life. "You a lying ass nigga!" I shouted with my guards up. "You ain't even have the audacity to tell me that you used to fuck with Luis' daughter!" I swung a hard right hook, Ken weaved my punch and slapped the shit out of me.

I was used to his slaps. I felt it, but they no longer hurt. I jumped up and came at him with everything I had. I wasn't wind-milling like most chicks when they fought, nah, I was straight from the shoulders with mine. Ken stopped swinging, I caught him once in the nose. Instead of slapping the shit out of me, he just shoved me to the floor. He stood over the floor and shouted, "I'm sorry, okay!"

I tried to get back up, but he only pushed me back down. I kept trying to get up, but he held me down with the palm of his hand on my head. I was pissed that I couldn't get past his hand. "You're not sorry, you're just sorry that you got caught!" I shouted as Ken walked away and sat on the edge of the bed.

"Hit me all you want—I'm not going to hit you back or stop you," he said as he looked sad on the edge of the bed.

I stood up with my fist balled up. I punched him so hard his lip started bleeding. I jumped back, hands up, ready for a fight. He shocked me. His reaction was to just taste his own blood. I put my hands down, there was no fun in fighting someone that wasn't going to fight back.

Ken lowered his head. When he raised it, he was crying. I had never seen him cry before. His tears melted the ice in my heart. I walked between his legs and raised his head so our eyes could meet. There was a glimmer there, a little hope.

"Kelvin, he was my way out the game. My first kid, my son." He cried then said, "The game took him away from me."

I brought his face to my stomach. We were both bleeding, and hurting emotionally. "Did you love her?" I asked.

"Of course, but it was way before I ever met you," he answered.

"Do you still love her?" I asked softly. I was afraid of his answer.

"I will always have love for her, Angel. She was the mother of my child. But what I had for her washed away when I met you. I could never love anyone the way I love you."

I felt his words. I hated the way he made me feel. He could make me feel like the luckiest woman in the world at times, then the next minute he would make me feel worthless, like I was nothing, the scum of the earth. I honestly wished he would've told me all of this before I felt that I couldn't trust him anymore.

Reluctantly, I wiped his tears with the palm of my hand. He looked into my eyes as I kissed his lips. I hated myself for loving him so much. A part of me wanted to protect him, love him, and ride for him. My mind was confusing my heart, and my heart was refusing to listen to my gut. I was in a lose-lose situation.

"My trial starts tomorrow. I-I—" he started saying, but I placed my finger to his lips.

I wasn't trying to think about his trial. He didn't know the outcome, but I did. Knowing that he was going to prison for the rest of his life, I wanted to remember this night for as long as I could.

I took a step back and lowered my shoulder strap to my bodysuit. I pulled it down, exposing my twins. Ken looked at me in shock. I could tell that his head was all over the place, but there was only one head I was concerned about right now. I stripped down to nothing. We traded places with me laying on my back and him standing straight in front of me. Ken stood there, as if he was seeing me naked for the very first time.

"Are you just going to stand there, or are you going to fuck this pussy?" I asked.

Ken chuckled. He stood over me and tried to kiss me. I pushed his head away. "No foreplay, just plain ol' fuckin'." I was calling the shots now.

Ken stripped down to nothing. He stood tall between my legs as he pushed them apart with his knees. As his dick neared my slit, I held my breath. Ken eased his overgrown dick inside of me. My ass was hanging off the bed, which allowed him to fuck me with everything he had.

Ken started off slow, until I said, "If you want to make love, then call Rain. Fuck me hard or put your dick up, nigga!"

I have heard before to be careful what you wish for. 'Cause I got what I wanted. Ken pulled his hard dick out and lined it back up with my slippery slit. He rammed all nine of his long hard inches inside of me with one thrust. I gasped and grunted as he did it over and over again. I could feel his thick veins as they rubbed up against my walls. His plump head felt like it was pushing up against my uterus. The feeling of his balls slapping my juicy sex lips with each stroke was breathtaking. I told him to fuck me, and fuck me he did.

"This what you wanted, huh!" Ken grunted as he pounded my pussy.

I slapped him hard and said, "No talking! Jus-just fuck me!" I didn't want to hear his voice. I just wanted to feel him inside of me.

I hated how God made a woman's body succumb to a

man's dick. The way a man's dick seemed more dominant and harder than a woman's vagina. No matter how tough a woman seemed, the dick always won in the end.

"Ahh . . . yes! Ahh . . . fuck!" I moaned as I grounded my pelvis into him, meeting him stroke for stroke.

Ken bit his bottom lip as he leaned forward and took my right nipple into his mouth. That shit felt so damn good, but I couldn't let him win this battle, so I pushed his head away. "Fuck me, harder!" I demanded.

"Arghh, shit!" Ken groaned as skin slapped skin. He was pumping his dick inside of me like he had something to prove. "I love this pussy," he said as he flexed his muscles.

I slapped him again. This time he grabbed my hands and pinned them over my head. I wrapped my legs around his waist and held on for the ride. The final ride!

11

EMMANUEL

I knocked lightly on Judge Simpson's chamber door. Judge Simpson opened the door and invited me in. I knew Judge Simpson personally. I had won numerous cases in her courtroom. "Emmanuel, what can I do for you?" Judge Simpson asked as she sat behind her desk. I sat opposite her desk and sighed deeply.

"I would like to withdraw my counsel from this case."

Judge Simpson took off her glasses and laid them on her desk. "Am I hearing myself correctly? Emmanuel Stevens is backing out of a case!"

"It's not just—" I wanted to tell her exactly what happened. My phone vibrated in my pocket. I pulled it out and looked at the screen. There was a text message from a random number. I clicked on the message. A picture of a gun was attached to the message. The test read, '*Hope you're not having cold feet. If you are, I hope this heats you up.*' There was also a gun emoji, with a clapping hand emoji.

I stood up quickly and looked around. "Emmanuel, are you okay?" Judge Simpson asked.

I placed my phone back in my pocket and looked around Judge Simpson's office. It was like Angel was watching me from the clouds. "I-I'm okay. You know what, forget we even had this conversation." I started for the door.

"Emmanuel, are you sure you're okay?" Judge Simpson asked.

I held on to the doorknob and said, "I really don't have a choice."

———

Angel

THE RIDE UP the elevator was quiet and awkward. Ken, me and Squirrel were at the Earl Campbell Federal courthouse for Ken's first day of trial. It was hell trying to get in the building. News reporters damn near tackled us when we got out of the car. I knew Ken was known all around Dallas, but people were acting like he was Donald Trump going to trial.

My phone rang in the quiet elevator. I looked at the screen. It was Bull for the umpteenth time. His worrisome ass had been blowing up my phone all damn night. He kept texting me, '9-1-1 answer'. I wanted to answer, but me and Ken were too busy wrestling naked.

I sent Bull to voicemail, then slipped my phone back in my purse. Squirrel looked at me and smiled. His golds were on public display. I swear I hated his ass with a passion. Especially when he smiled.

The elevator opened. I stepped off first. The hallway outside the courtroom was packed. A bunch of people were there to support Ken, and the rest were there hoping he went away for-ever.

"Kendrick Watson, how do you feel about your first day of trial? Do you feel confident? Do you feel that your drug dealing money can buy your freedom?" Channel Five news bombarded Ken with question after question.

"Kendrick Watson—" The newscaster started again before Ken cut him off.

"I'm not a *drug dealer*, and I feel that by the end of my trial I'll be able to prove it to you and the city of Dallas." Ken smiled for the cameras.

"Mr. Watson, some people say that you're more dangerous than your uncle, Percy Watson," Channel Eleven said.

Ken laughed and said, "My uncle was never a violent man. And neither am I."

"Kendrick! Kendrick!" CNN news chased after us as Squirrel moved them out of our path like a bodyguard.

My phone started ringing again. I felt it ring as Ken looked at me. "You're not going to answer that, it could be important," he said.

"It's not more important than you. I'll answer it later."

"Handle yo' business, I'm cool. It could be Luis, remember," Ken said with one eyebrow raised.

I was supposed to get my first shipment today. I nodded at Ken. "Let me check—I'll meet you inside," I said as I walked to the ladies' room.

As soon as I got inside the ladies' room, I dialed Bull's number and waited for him to answer. He finally answered on the fifth ring, like he wasn't expecting my call. "Why haven't you been answering yo' damn phone!" Bull shouted as soon as I answered the phone.

I pulled the phone away from my ear and looked at the screen. He couldn't have been talking to me. Not Angel! "First of all, lower yo' fuckin' tone when you're talkin' to me. Recognize who the fuck you're dealing with, okay!" I said without raising my voice.

Bull huffed and said, "I've been calling you since last night."

"Okay, and!" I was getting annoyed with him already. Niggas didn't know how to play their position.

"It's about Turtle," he mumbled.

"Okay, and did you get the job done?" I looked for an empty stall.

"I was, but." He huffed again.

"But what?" I didn't like the way he said *but*.

"Bishop and his crew got to him first," he said.

"What!" I couldn't have heard him right.

"Bishop and his crew—they kidnapped him right when I was about to gun him down," he explained.

I sat on the toilet, not believing what I was hearing. "Are you sure it was Bishop?"

"Positive! I saw his face, and he saw mine." Bull sounded like he was nervous.

"Okay, calm down," I said as I tried to gather my thoughts together. "Did Bishop say anything to you?" I asked.

"Naw'l, he saw me, but I don't think he knew exactly

who I was or he would've gunned me down or took me too."

"Fuck! Okay, do they got Turtle? Do you think they killed him?"

"I doubt it," he said. "They killed all of his men, they just snatched Turtle up alone."

Damn. I thought to myself. They were probably trying to use Turtle to get something out of Ken. But why haven't they contacted Ken yet was the question.

"Okay, look. Keep your mouth shut. As of now Ken knows nothing of the kidnapping. I'm at the courthouse, I'll call you once we leave!" I said as I walked out the stall.

"I'm pulling up to the courthouse as we speak. I'll see you in the courtroom." I could hear car horns in the background of his phone.

The restroom door cracked open. Ken stuck his head inside and said, "Babe, are you finished? Trial's about to start." I could see the stress all over his face.

I hung the phone up and turned the volume all the way down. Ken smiled at me. I knew it was hurting him to smile knowing deep down he was afraid of the *what if*. Little did he know, his whole world was about to come crashing down on his head.

———

Ken

I WALKED down the aisle with my wife right behind me. The courtroom was filled to capacity. I knew the majority of the people in the audience. Some were friends, most were haters waiting to see me fall.

I walked past the swinging door and stood beside Emmanuel and his secretary. Emmanuel was sweating like he was nervous, like he was the one on trial. "Are you okay?" I asked him.

Emmanuel gave me a half smile and said, "Shouldn't I be asking you that?"

I smiled at his sense of humor. For some odd reason, Emmanuel looked at Angel and his smile faded. As fast as he looked at her, the faster he looked away. The bailiff walked in front of the courtroom and addressed the audience. "I ask that all cellphones be turned off, no pictures, no talking, and please remain seated."

The judge's chamber door opened. The bailiff said, "All Rise!" The entire audience stood up. "I present Honorable Judge Simpson." Judge Simpson took her seat.

The bailiff lowered his hand and said, "You may all be seated."

Everyone took their seats. I unbuttoned the two buttons on my Italian suit and took my seat. Emmanuel and the United States District Attorney walked up to the podium. I couldn't make out what the judge was saying. Emmanuel and the DA nodded and they both walked back to their tables.

Emmanuel leaned over to me and whispered, "Today we're going to have our open statements, present all evidence, and then put in any motions you want me to file."

I nodded.

The District Attorney was a woman. A Black woman at that. She looked to be in her early thirties. Brown-skinned with a nice shape. She wore a white button-down shirt that was tucked into her black knee-length skirt. She walked in front of the room and addressed the jury.

There were twelve people seated in the jury booth. Six of them the DA handpicked, and the other six Emmanuel picked. I couldn't tell which were his and which were hers. But I can bet my freedom that the six whites were picked by the DA.

"Ladies and gentleman of the jury," the DA started off with. "First of all, I would like to personally thank you for taking time out of your busy day to help the state of Texas put away a man that has polluted our sweet state with poison."

I looked down. I knew this was about to be one hell of a trial. The DA walked closer to the jury box and continued. "The man that you see here today, Kendrick Rodrick Watson. The man in the high-dollar fancy Italian suit," she said as she pointed her pretty manicured nails at me. "He didn't get that suit by working an honest nine-to-five like you and me. He got it by hurting people, murdering people —" she said as Emmanuel cut her off.

"Objection, Your Honor!" Emmanuel shouted. "My client is not on trial for murder."

I nodded and held my smile in.

"Sustained! DA, let's stick to the reason we're here," Judge Simpson said.

The DA nodded and continued. "Kendrick Watson is sitting in front of you, not for being an outstanding citizen. No, Kendrick Watson is sitting in front of you for making millions of dollars by force-feeding people narcotics, cocaine. I say force-feed because after a thorough test of the cocaine we found, which was found with his finger prints on it, it came back to 85%. You know what that means? It was 15% from being pure cocaine. Kendrick had the kind of cocaine that would make a hard working mother of four turn into a prostitute who neglects her children. Kendrick had the kind of product that takes food from innocent children's mouths. Kendrick Watson may be sitting here in front of you looking scared, innocent. Please, don't let the look fool you! That look is the look a man gives you when he knows he's been caught. I ask you. Hungry kids ask you. Mothers suffering from continuous relapse are begging you. Get this man off the street! Thank you!" the DA said and walked by me to her seat.

I looked at Emmanuel. Emmanuel picked up a glass and filled it to the rim with water. He gulped the water down, then he stood up. He buttoned his suit jacket up, then he nodded at me. Let the games begin!

12

EMMANUEL

As I listened to the DA's opening arguments, I was very impressed. For her to be so young, she sounded like she knew what she was doing. Not like it was hard to get a conviction with concrete evidence. As she finished, I stood to my feet. Kendrick looked at me and gave me a half smile. I knew he was thinking I better show him why he paid me all that money. I looked back at his wife, Angel. She made a gun with her fingers, reminding me of the inevitable. Being honest, her lil evil ass actually scares me.

I walked around the table and addressed the jury. "Ladies and gentlemen of the jury. I come before you today to present to you a man. Kendrick Rodrick Watson. The state of Texas and the federal court system will try to paint you the picture of Kendrick being a villain. A menace to society. A drug dealer. A homewrecker. What I will do is tell you the truth of who Kendrick Watson really is."

I walked back and forth with my hands behind my back. "Kendrick Watson is a man that attended grade school like you and I. Kendrick didn't fall victim like most kids from his neighborhood. No, Kendrick was smarter than that. Kendrick took the road less traveled and graduated high school. On the road to college, Kendrick had a full scholarship to Texas state. He had a promising future in college basketball, and a hopeful future in the NBA. Kendrick's dream was crushed by a stray bullet that was intended for another person. So, you're not looking at a repeat offender. You're looking at a man who's tried to make a life for himself. So what if he wears fancy Italian suits?" The jury laughed.

"Kendrick Watson is a man who's been robbed of a very promising future. Don't be the bullet that will rob him of the rest of his life. Give him something that was robbed from him at a young age. A chance. Thank you!"

I nodded to the jury as I walked back to the table to take my seat. Kendrick leaned into me and whispered, "That was nice, but you know I never played basketball, or I never had a scholarship to Texas state."

"It's not what you know, it's about what you can prove in court."

———

Angel

AFTER COURT, everyone was invited back to the house for a small get-together. Ken invited Emmanuel and his secretary, but Emmanuel denied the invitation politely. His pale skin ass secretary kept sneaking ugly glances at me. I put on my best smile and blew her white ass a kiss.

When we made it home, Ken turned the charcoal grill on as I took some ribs, steaks, ball parks, and some thick sliced turkey bologna from the d-freezer. People started showing up like we were having a party. That was the whole plan though. We knew the feds would be watching, so Ken came up with a plan to throw them off. In the beginning the feds would see Ken in the backyard grilling. An hour or so later Ken would sneak away to the secret location Luis delivered the ki's to.

I played host as always. The happy, loving, ride or die wife. Every time the doorbell rang, I answered it, just to make sure the feds were taking pictures, and knowing they were, I was always in them, being seen answering the door.

I answered the door, my two sisters were smiling at me. "Jas! Chelsea'!" I screamed their names and smiled. "What are y'all doing here?" I asked excitedly as I let them in.

"You know I couldn't let you go through this alone," Chelsea said. Chelsea, whose nickname was Chels', was my oldest sister. Chels' was light-skinned as hell. Fairly tall, about five-foot-eight inches. She had freckles on her cheek and hands that made her look mixed. Long, curly, dirty blonde hair that she kept in a puff ball ponytail. She was once a skinny brat, but once she had my nephew she sprouted into a thick chick. Now she's thicker than a snicker.

Now my other sister, Jasmine, she's my bitch. All my life I've had a small sense of jealousy for her. Plus, she's smart. Jas' is a registered nurse. She's the good sister, the quiet one.

As my sisters walked in the house, I kissed them both on the cheek. "I'm glad y'all came. I could use some support." As soon as they saw Jas and Chels', the niggas all started shooting their shots. Chelsea stopped as one of Ken's homies started spitting game to her. I butted in their conversation and said, "She's married." Chelsea gave me a salty look.

"Damn, bitch, what are you? The marriage police or som'?" Chelsea joked. I smiled at her comment and pulled her into the kitchen.

"So, how'd it go today?" Jas' asked as she leaned over the counter and grabbed an apple from the fruit bowl.

Before I could speak, someone said, "Damn, ma. I'd love to be that apple right now." It was Smurf, Ken's godson. I thought for sure Jas' was about to curse his ass out.

Instead, Jas' looked up at him and blushed. I shook my head. That was why us country girls should always stay in the country. Jas' was looking at him like he was the apple. She stared at his Lil Fiz looking ass in complete lust. Smurf walked up to Jas', he took the apple from her hand, then he bit it where her mouth had just been. Jas' looked at me and Chelsea with her mouth wide open.

"I don't know what it is, but this is the best apple I've ever tasted," Smurf said as he gave the apple back. "I'm Smurf, and you are?" he asked.

Jas' looked at me again as if she couldn't remember her own name. "Jas-Jasmine, right?" she muttered as she looked at me for clarification. Chelsea broke out in laughter. I couldn't do nothing but shake my head.

Don't get me wrong, Smurf was very handsome. He

had long hair, kinda like Chelsea's. He was light-skinned with tats all over his body, some even on his face. Smurf was only twenty years old. Close to my age, but too damn young for me. I loved older boss niggas. Plus, he was Pistol's son. Pistol was Ken's older cousin. Pistol was a straight thug. Everything he did was gangsta. He was a big homie in Oak Cliff, a known blood, and a certified killa. He had been to prison twice for murder. Each time he only served nothing more than ten years because Ken would make sure he had the best defense attorneys. Seeing that the Lil Fiz look alike was here, his father couldn't be too far behind.

"Smurf, where's your pops? Is he here?" I asked.

Smurf smiled, letting his dimples pop out at Jas', then Smurf said, "Yeah, he's here. He's in the backyard with Big Ken."

"Oh my God! Smurf, this is my big sister Jas'. Jas', this is Kendrick's Godson, Smurf." I introduced them. I was tired of them acting like they were the only two in the room.

Jas' looked at me like I had put her on the spot. Now the bitch had some common sense. Smurf leaned into Jas' and started whispering some sweet nothings into her ear. Jas' started laughing like he was a stand-up comedian. I fanned them off and walked in the backyard with Chelsea right behind me.

As soon as me and Chelsea got outside, Chelsea did her best NuNu impersonation. "Oh boy, that is my jam!" She popped her legs as she sang with the song. I shook my head laughing at her crazy ass. I looked around for Ken. He was

nowhere in sight. I shook my head. Not only did he shake
the feds, but me too.

———

Ken

"GO AROUND THE BLOCK AGAIN," I commanded Squirrel.

Squirrel laughed and said, "Big Ken, them pigs ain't
even see us leave, so how could they be following us?"

"Just in case," I said as I looked at my cousin, Pistol.

"Good to see you, family. How long you in town for?" I
asked. Pistol was born and raised in Dallas, but all his life
he's been under the DPD microscope, so he decided to
move to Houston to get out of the limelight.

"Just a few days until your trial is over." He looked at
me and said, "Why? Do you need me to stay awhile?"

I nodded. "I might. Depends on the outcome of the
trial."

Pistol nodded as we pulled up to one of my many ware-
houses. This one location was my favorite. The traffic on
Harry Hines was always frequent, so no one ever really
paid any attention to us, and I paid the Hispanics to look
after my shit by buying them a tire shop right next door.

"I haven't been to this spot in a while," Pistol said,
smiling. He knew what it meant to come to this specific
location. Money time.

Squirrel parked as Filipe and Jorge let the garage down.
I stepped out of the truck and embraced Luis' most trusted
soldiers. "Filipe, Jorge! I'm glad you two could make it."

Jorge nodded. "Traffic was a bum," he said as he

escorted me to a U-Haul van that I had got accustomed to seeing.

Jorge and Filipe were alone. There was no use of having multiple shooters with them. Luis only dealt with people that were family, people he trusted. And he only delivered the product once he received his payment. Filipe unlocked the lock on the back of the U-Haul and raised the door. Inside the van were boxes and boxes of flour tortillas. Filipe climbed inside with Jorge right behind him. Filipe punched in a code on his phone and a secret department opened up in the back of the van. I climbed in the back of the U-Haul, looked past Filipe and Jorge, and smiled. I rubbed my hands together as Jorge handed me two kilos of cocaine. I kissed the ki's and tossed them to Pistol. This went on until there was a hundred and ten kilos on a wooden pallet.

I jumped out the U-Haul and counted the bricks again. Once I finished, I looked at Jorge and Filipe confused. "Jorge, you do know there's an extra ten ki's, right? I only ordered a hundred."

Jorge nodded and said, "Si, Senor Luis said to take the extra ten as a going away present, for your loyalty."

I smiled as I shook Filipe's hand as well as Jorge's. I offered to pay them for their drive, but they refused as always. I knew they were just loyal to Luis; whatever he asked of them, they would do it. Filipe locked the U-Haul back and said, "Keep your head high, hombre."

"There's no other way," I said, smiling. I shook Jorge's hand again as they departed like they were never there.

"This is a lot of ma'fuckin' dope," Pistol said.

I looked at the stack of bricks; indeed, it was a lot, but dealing with my uncle Turtle, I had seen tons at one time.

I cleared my throat and said, "I had to make a move to keep the family fed while I'm away. Just because one soldier dies that doesn't mean the war's over with." I grabbed a brick of cocaine and looked at it. It was crazy how the dope was made to make some niggas, and at the same time break some niggas.

"How do you want to do it, same as last time?" Squirrel asked, ready to distribute the dope. Squirrel was a true hustler. A dedicated soldier, a rider; that's why it was hard for me to tell him that Angel would be taking my spot once I went away. It wasn't that I didn't trust Squirrel, or any other soldier in the gang. I trusted them all with my life. I can honestly say I knew why I chose Angel to take my spot. Control. It was control, and power. With Angel in position, I would still have the power, and control of the streets. With my queen in position, I would always have a throne to come home to.

"For now, you take a ki, and Pistol you take one, on me. The other eight, Squirrel, take them to Bull. The rest, we'll lock up here until next week. I don't want to put all the eggs in one basket, feel me?"

They both nodded. They both grabbed a ki from the pallet. I grabbed a dolly and lined it up with the pallet, then I rolled the dolly under the pallet. I wheeled the pallet into the back office, then into the closet where I had a closet size safe. My office was bullet-proof and secured by a code that only I knew. Well, and Angel, only because it was her birthday as the code.

I wheeled the pallet into the safe and closed the door

behind me. I locked it and placed the code in and turned the knob. I stopped briefly to gather my thoughts. Life was moving so fast, yet it felt like it was moving backwards instead of forwards. I turned around and looked at my guys. What I would do to go back in time and not sell that rat that dope! Sad thing, there was no going back in time, so I just had to do the time.

13

EMMANUEL

When Kendrick invited me to his house to enjoy some good ol' barbeque, I almost went, until I saw his wife standing behind him. I didn't want to be around her no more than I had to, so I declined his offer.

Standing in my office, pacing back and forth for the past hour, Janice finally told me to sit my black ass down. She said I was making her nervous. I don't understand how. It wasn't like it was her fingerprints on a murder weapon. I did sit down though, until my mind started racing again.

"What if—" I shouted as I jumped up. Janice looked at me. "What if we break into Kendrick's house and steal the gun back. That way, Angel won't have anything over my head. I could finish the trial, and somehow keep Kendrick out of prison, or at least help him get some time he could do.

Janice nodded and said, "Sounds like a damn good plan, if you were a crook." She laughed. "Emmanuel, you don't know anything about breaking and entering, and neither do I."

"I know a little. I represented some of the world's greatest bandits. Some have actually told me how they did it. Come on, Janice, I really need your help on this. Please!" I begged.

Janice sighed. "Okay, but if we do go to jail, whenever we get out I want an all-expenses paid trip to the Bahamas." I smiled and nodded.

———

I WATCHED from my car as I watched the feds watch Kendrick's house. I wasn't sure if Kendrick or his evil ass wife were home, but I had to try my luck; hell, it was already running out.

I pulled my car around the back of the house. I parked and looked over to Janice. She looked beyond scared. Hell, I was too. "What if they catch us and kill us?" Janice said, scared.

"Shh-hh, don't talk like that. For all we know they might not even be home. I didn't see Kendrick's car in the driveway."

Janice nodded. I turned the car off and emptied my pockets. I stepped out of the car and walked around. The cool night air hit me in the face. I could still smell charcoal in the air. Janice stood beside me, then looked at me as if she was waiting on me to make the first move.

"You sure they're not inside?" she said,

"Janice, if this was your last week being free, would

you spend it in the house?" I asked. Janice shook her head. "Exactly!"

I walked to the back gate of Kendrick's mini mansion. I looked around for a 'beware of dogs' sign. Once I found none, I looked back to Janice and said, "Okay, you go first."

"Why do I have to go first?" she said.

"Because, if I go first, who's going to help you get over?"

"Ease yourself do—" I started to say as Janice leaped over and hit the ground hard.

"Ughh!" she grunted. I hurried and climbed over the fence to see if she was okay.

"Janice, are you okay?" I asked as I kneeled down beside her.

"I'm okay. I think I just knocked the wind out of myself." I laughed as I helped her to her feet.

I brushed the dirt from her clothes and looked at the house. "I don't see a light on inside, so if we hurry, we can be in and out before anyone gets back." I walked off with Janice behind me in pain. I stood at Kendrick's back door. I could see directly inside his house from the patio door.

"How are we going to get inside without triggering the alarm?" Janice asked. I stayed silent as I looked around. I really didn't have a plan. What I wanted to do, before the nosey feds fucked up my entire plan, was to look under the front doormat and see if they had a spare key like most people with money do. But since that plan is a no-brainer, I had to improvise.

I looked around for anything I would've thought to hide a key in or under. Not that Angel or Kendrick were smart enough to think like me, but yeah. I looked at the ground. By the swing set sat a flower pot with a single rose growing from the roots. I picked the small pot up and smiled. A single key.

I held the key up like I had just found the cure for cancer. I walked to the backdoor. I looked around, making sure there weren't any cameras. For Kendrick to be a drug lord, I was surprised to find he had no security cameras. I placed the key in the lock, closed my eyes, and silently prayed that I didn't get sent to hell for what I was about to do.

I twisted the key and turned the doorknob. Angel's scent flooded my nose as soon as I opened the door. I stood still for a second, just in case they had a guard dog. Janice leaned over my shoulder and scared the hell out of me.

"Are we really going to break into a client's house?" she asked.

I stepped inside the house and said, "It's a little too late for that." I walked completely inside and left Janice at the door for her to decide her own fate.

The only light on inside the house was a lamp beside the couch. A noise came from behind me. I turned to see Janice standing behind me with a statue in her hand. "I had one of these in college," she said, smiling with the statue in her hand.

"Put that shit down. Fingerprints, remember." Janice poked her lips out. Even though I spoke to her harshly, I was glad that she decided to come in. Her coming in meant she had my back, no matter what.

I looked around for the gun. I looked high and low. With all of my searching, I came up empty-handed. I was afraid to go upstairs, just in case Angel or Kendrick was up there asleep. And I didn't want to wake a sleeping demon. But I had no choice. There was a big chance that the gun was in fact upstairs.

I crept up the stairs with Janice right on my tail. There were four rooms up the stairs. A bathroom in the hallway. What looked to be two guest rooms, and a master bedroom. I was glad to see that Angel or Kendrick wasn't home. I was free to search the house without being scared.

"Okay, you search the room down the hall, and I'll search the master bedroom," I instructed.

Janice placed both of her hands on her hips and said, "Why do I have to search the room down the hall? Why can't we just stick together? What if one of them comes home, then what?" she said, making a lot of sense.

"Okay, just stay close to me, and don't touch nothing that you don't have to touch," I said as I led the way inside the master bedroom.

Their master bedroom was nice, much bigger than mine. Made me think that I should've charged Kendrick more than what I had. It took me and Janice to raise the mattress. The only reason that I chose to check under the mattress was because I saw it once in this movie called, *Four Brothers*. In the movie, that is where they hid their guns. I guess that's only in the movies, because there were no guns there.

Janice checked in the clothes drawer, and I checked in the night stand beside the bed. As I opened the drawer, I got excited. "Yes!" I shouted.

Janice walked beside me and asked, "Is that it?"

As soon as she asked the question, I then realized that

the gun we were staring at wasn't the gun we were in fact looking for. "Dammit! This isn't it, the gun isn't this big. The gun she had was much smaller." I slammed the drawer out of frustration. A noise came in from downstairs.

I heard the front door close, followed by laughter. I tried to be as still as possible to make sure I wasn't hearing things. "Did you hear that?" Janice asked. I nodded. "Manny, they're here!" she said, panicking. Janice looked around like there was a secret door she could sneak out of.

I crept towards the door. The sound of Kendrick's voice got closer. "Quick, get under the bed!" Janice looked at me with fear in her eyes. "Now, go!" I said as I gave her a little push.

Janice squeezed under the large bed as I went under right behind her. Kendrick and Angel burst through the door as they tried to outkiss each other. Angel shoved Kendrick on the bed. She pulled his pants down and sunk to her knees right in front of us. Janice looked over at me. I held my finger to my lips as I listened to the sound of Angel perform oral surgery on Kendrick's dick.

Kendrick started moaning. "Uhmm! Suck that dick, babe! Just like that!" Angel gasped as she came up for air. Her dress fell to her feet as she stepped out of it. Kendrick sat up as he pulled his clothes all the way off. He eased to the edge of the bed. Angel kept her heels on, but stepped out of her Victoria Secret thong. She straddled him backwards.

The bed started to shake as their moans invaded the room. Angel's legs disappeared, then her hands appeared. She scared the shit out of me. Kendrick stood to his feet, as Angel fell to the floor with her hands holding her for support. Luckily, her eyes were closed or she would've most definitely seen us.

In my mind I kept saying, '*Beat that pussy up, keep her eyes close*'. All I could hear was Kendrick grunting, and Angel moaning. Kendrick picked Angel up without missing a beat. The way they were performing, it looked as if they were auditioning for a role in one of Zane's erotica movies. Their weight came down hard on the bed. I couldn't tell who was on top, but the way they were going at it, I thought for sure they were fucking like it would be their last time.

I looked over to Janice to assure her everything would be okay, but when I looked at her she left me in complete shock. Her eyes were closed. She was biting her bottom lip as she fingered her clit. I shook my head and thought, '*White women*'.

Ken

I LOOKED around the courtroom for my uncle Turtle. This made the second court date straight; he was a no-show. I started to call him to make sure he was okay, but I figured the feds were monitoring my calls.

The bailiff walked up to the defense table and whispered to me. "If Mr. Stevens does not show in the next ten minutes we'll have to reschedule for tomorrow."

I nodded and said, "Okay." I looked at my watch. Emmanuel was over forty-five minutes late. He was supposed to be in court at eight o'clock; it was now eight forty-five. I only hoped he had a legit reason for being late. I was paying him too much money for him to not show up.

"Angel stood up and leaned over the wooden swinging doors. "Do you want me to call him? He could be having car trouble, or he could be stuck in traffic."

I huffed. "Please, bae. The bailiff said if he's not here in the next ten minutes we'll have to reschedule for tomorrow."

Angel nodded. "I'll be right back, babe." As soon as she turned to walk away, the doors to the courtroom opened. Emmanuel and his secretary rushed to the defense table.

Emmanuel looked as if he hadn't got a lick of sleep last night. He had bags under his eyes that made him look twice his age. His secretary's hair was a mess. They looked as if they had just got done having sex. Emmanuel sat his briefcase down on the table and said, "Sorry I'm late."

I laughed lightly. Emmanuel smelled as if had slept in someone's attic. "Are you okay?" I asked him.

He nodded and said, "Never better." I looked at his clothes. He looked as if he had got them from the bottom of a clothes hamper.

"You sure? We can reschedule if you want to. You look like you're not feeling well!" I said.

Emmanuel opened his briefcase with a little aggression. "I said I'm fine." He sighed, then said, "I just want to get this over with so we both can move on with our lives."

"Me too. The sooner the better. The sooner the jury makes a decision, the quicker I can plan out my future," I said.

"Are you sure?" Emmanuel asked.

"Am I sure what?"

"Are you sure you're ready to get this over with? Are you not afraid of the outcome?" he asked me.

I shook my head and said, "Whatever happens, happens. It's better to get it over with than to prolong the inevitable."

"Okay, you asked for it," Emmanuel said as the bailiff stood in front of the courtroom.

"All rise!" the bailiff said as Judge Simpson walked out of her chamber. Everyone in attendance stood up. As the judge took her seat, the bailiff instructed us all to take ours, then he walked off and took his position beside the podium.

Emmanuel raised his hand and asked the judge if he could approach her. Judge Simpson agreed.

Emmanuel walked up to the judge with the DA right behind him. They spoke in a hush tone. The judge nodded, looking at me. The DA shook her head and said something back to Emmanuel. The whole scene didn't look good from my point of view.

I looked to the side of me to Emmanuel's secretary. "What's going on up there?" I asked her.

She shook her head and said, "I can't tell." She looked at a few papers, then said, "Kendrick, I don't know you from Adam, but you seem like a decent guy. I don't know why I'm telling you this, but you can't trust every human God created, because even God's most favorite creation turned against him."

I didn't know what that had to do with anything, but I still nodded. Emmanuel walked towards our table and stood behind it. The DA walked back to her table and stood behind it. Emmanuel looked at me and said, "Stand up."

I stood to my feet and asked, "What just happened up there?"

"You just got your wish," was all Emmanuel said.

Judge Simpson looked at me and said, Kendrick Watson, do you understand what you're asking for?"

I looked at Emmanuel, wondering what I should say. Emmanuel nodded. I looked back to the judge and said, "Yes, ma'am. I understand."

Judge Simpson tilted her glasses and said, "The jury should note that Kendrick Watson changed his plea of not guilty to *guilty*. He's asking for mercy from the courtroom, and leniency from the jury. Sentencing phase will be held tomorrow at eight thirty, court is dismissed." Judge Simpson banged her gavel.

I looked at Emmanuel and punched him right in his face.

14

ANGEL

Jas' and Smurf kept me company as we waited in my red Volkswagen convertible. We've been waiting in the Dallas County parking lot for Kendrick to be released from jail. Yes, I said jail. After Ken punched his lawyer, the police took him into custody for simple assault. I can't lie, the whole scene was funny as fuck. When the judge told Ken that the sentencing phase would be tomorrow, all the color in Ken's face drained. I sat in the front pew doing my best not to laugh. I damn near drew blood from my cheeks trying my hardest not to laugh.

I got a text from Cowboys Bail-bonds that Ken should be released in the next thirty minutes to an hour. I should've left his ass in there, hell. He'll have to get used to it come tomorrow.

"Angel, what are you going to do with Ken?" my sister Jas' asked as her and Smurf cuddled in the backseat.

I don't even know why I introduced them. Since the barbeque, they've been inseparable. "I'm going to love him and hold him down. That's my duty as his wife!" I said with a straight face. I told her a bold face lie, only because Smurf was in the car.

"Girl, love don't love nobody." Jas' laughed as she looked at Smurf.

"So, you don't believe in love?" Smurf asked Jas'.

"Love is just an emotion. It comes and goes, like fear, or any other emotion!" Jas' said.

Smurf tickled her. I looked at them through the rearview mirror and smiled. They reminded me of me and Ken when we first met. "So you don't think I'm capable of loving you? Smurf asked as he made her squirm.

Jas' couldn't stop laughing as he continued to tickle her. Her legs kicked the back of my seat. Tears began to fall from her eyes as she kicked. "Okay! Okay, please!" she begged.

Smurf laughed as he finally gave her a breather. Jas' fixed her clothes and said, "I'm not saying that you're not capable of loving me, 'cause I am lovable in every way. What I'm saying is, love is like joy. It comes and goes. It's just another emotion. You feel it for a moment, then it passes over you."

I sat in the driver's seat with my foot in my lap as I listened to Jas' explain her definition of love. Me and Chelsea always thought that Jas' was a pushover, but hearing her now, she proved me wrong. She deserved more credit than we gave her.

"What do you think, queen? You think love is surreal?" Smurf asked me.

My phone buzzed with a text. It was from Bull, again. I smiled. Bull was sweet and consistent. That was why I kinda gave him the time of day. Bull sent me a text saying that he missed my smile. How he keeps having dreams of kissing my juicy lips. That when the judge bangs her gavel again there will be nothing or no one to stand in our way. He also sent a bunch of heart emojis. Gangsters!

"I'm not going to just say that love is just an emotion. But, I will say that there are two kinds of love," I said as I texted Bull back, then sat my phone in the cup holder.

"Come on now, queen." Smurf laughed. "Now I can see why you two are sisters. How the hell are there two kinds of love?" Smurf asked as he massaged Jas' legs as they rested on his lap.

"Okay, let me explain. You have, *being-in-love*, and *falling-in-love*. See, what you feel for Jas' is *falling-in-love*. She can do no wrong in your eyes at the moment. It's like the newlywed stage."

Smurf nodded and said, "So, what's the *being-in-love* stage?"

I laughed. Smurf was like a kid in school, ready to learn. "Being-in-love is kinda what Jas' said. It's more of an emotion. But, *being-in-love* is saying that you love that person, but you're really just dealing with that person because you've invested so many years with that person."

"Wait!" Jas' said. "I'm confused. Those definitions sound like the same thing. How can there be two different kinds of love, when you described them as the exact same thing?"

"Because love is confusing," I said.

Smurf laughed and said, "You crazy, queen."

I smiled and thought, '*You have no idea*'.

Emmanuel

"OUCH!" I flinched as Janice held a pack of frozen peas to my swollen eye.

Janice popped my hand and said, "Hold still! This is the only way to get the swelling to go down." She placed the pack of frozen peas to my eye. I flinched again. She laughed. "Big baby!" She smiled and said, "He got you pretty good. I can still see his fist print on your face." She teased.

"So, that's funny! Okay, you're on restriction."

"Restriction? What kind?" she asked.

I snatched the peas from her and said, "Dick restriction!"

Janice jumped up and fell to her knees. "Noo! Not dick restriction! Anything but dick restriction, please!" She laughed.

I laughed, too. Janice was a totally different person from the Janice I met years ago. Since the day Hannah left, Janice has been the only thing in my life that's made any sense.

"You play too much, get up." I laughed as Janice got off the floor and stood beside me. "Thank you," I said seriously.

"For?" she replied.

"For being you. For breaking through the darkness with your light. I swear I couldn't have done this without you."

Janice kissed me. Her lips tasted like the Pineapple Martini she had been drinking. My dick jumped as Janice leaned over my lap. "Look what you've done. You woke him up." Janice looked at my lap and smiled. She licked her lips.

"Can I put him back to sleep?" she asked as she unzipped my pants and pulled my dick out. She sank to her knees in front of me. She pushed my legs apart aggressively, making my dick bob up and down. Janice grinned as she looked at my dick do the happy dance.

Janice looked at my dick for a long time. The way she looked, I thought she wasn't satisfied with what she was looking at. She spat on my dick aggressively. She looked at the way her saliva slid down my dick and she smiled. She spat again just as she took my dick into her mouth. Her spit dripped down her chin as she stared into my eyes. She stared into my eyes as I stared into hers.

Janice removed her hands. Bobbing her head up and down on my dick, she began to pull her sweats under her ass. She had an ass like CoCo. It sat up perfectly. The curve of it, the way it cupped. It was amazing.

As Janice tried to take her clothes off while giving me a blowjob with no hands, her hair started to get in the way. I showed her I could be a gentleman as I moved her hair out of the way.

"Seeing my dick go in and out of your mouth is so fuckin' sexy," I said as I rested my head on the back edge of the couch. On many occasions I had visions of Janice naked, me bending her over my office desk. Her skirt raised just above her ass. My dick bringing her to the most absolute bliss she's ever felt. I know I wasn't the only boss that's ever thought about having sex with their secretary. Especially one as bad as Janice.

Janice replied to my comment by locking her jaws on my dick. My eyes tightened up, and so did my ass. Janice knew how to suck a dick. When she told me she was the head of her class, I didn't believe her. Now, I'll never doubt her again. As she popped my dick out of her mouth, I was on the verge of cumming, and fast. I was glad she had stopped. She had me on the edge of Mars, climbing my way to heaven.

Janice stood up and stepped out of her thong. As I eased off the couch, I slid my pants down to my ankles. I was too excited to take them all the way off. "Bend over!" I demanded.

Janice bent over in front of me; she rested her hands on the coffee table in front of her. Her pretty pink pussy sat perfectly between her white toned legs. I gripped her upper thighs, right next to her love box.

"S-sss." She gasped as I spread her sex lips with the tip of my tongue. I cupped my tongue in her hole to slurp up all of her juices. "Damn, Manny, that feels so-ooo good." She moaned as I rubbed my face between her ass cheeks. It didn't take long for her to turn me out. I had never even stuck my nose between my own wife's ass. Ex-wife, that is. Janice had me doing shit I'd never done in my life. Damn white devil!

I sat back on the couch, legs spread. Janice turned around and straddled my lap, her back to me. She gripped my dick from the back, placing it at her entrance, and slowly eased down on the tip. "Uhhmmm, yes-ss!" She moaned as she eased past the tip.

Her pussy was so tight, I thought for sure she was a virgin. She did a trick, riding my dick backwards, showing me shit I'd never seen before. She spread her ass cheeks so that I could have front row seats to her show. And by God, it was the most beautiful sight I'd ever seen. My black dick invading her pretty pink pussy was like a painting from Picasso.

As she bounced up and down on my dick, she ran her fingers through her long blonde hair as she moaned, "Yes! Fuck, yes-ss!" I smacked her ass as she moaned.

Smacking her ass made a loud popping sound. My hand was imprinted in her ass cheeks as they turned red. Janice leaned forward, resting her hands on the coffee table. Her pussy opened up right before my eyes.

Pop! Pop! Pop! I smacked her cheeks. Left cheek, right cheek. I smacked her ass like I was popping a drum seat. "Oh God!" she yelled. "I'm cumming-ggg!" she yelled as she sat upright and slow-grind on my dick.

Janice closed her legs tight and began to bounce up and down on my pole like she was giving me a lap dance. I squeezed my eyes shut as I felt the cum building in my balls. I squeezed my ass cheeks and let my body relax inside of hers. Janice kept grinding as the tip of my dick became super sensitive. I leaned forward and placed soft kisses all over her back.

"Manny?" she said as she panted.

"Yes," I answered as I tried to catch my breath.

"After tomorrow, what do you think will happen?" she asked, then she stood up. My cum-soaked dick lay on my leg as Janice sat on my knee.

"Tomorrow, Kendrick will probably be sentenced to life, especially with him punching me in front of the jury like he did," I explained.

"Then what?"

"Then we take the money I have, move far away, and start all over," I said, trying to convince her and myself that everything will be okay.

Janice kissed my lips and said, "I was hoping you would say something like that."

15

KEN

"What's good y'all?" I greeted my most loyal soldiers. "I know it's late—"

Pistol laughed and said, "You think! It's three in the ma'fuckin' morning."

I laughed. "I know, but I caught the pigs asleep, so I had a chance to sneak out, so I did." I looked around the warehouse. I was surrounded by hittas, gangstas, my family —B.M.B. It seemed like it was yesterday I started B.M.B. Now it seemed like it was all over in just a blink of an eye.

"I called y'all niggas here so that everything will already be established for the team. As y'all should already know, unfortunately, I'll be sentenced tomorrow. Not sure how long, but I'm prepared for whatever they throw my way." Squirrel nodded at me with respect.

I stood at the head of the table as everyone else stood by ranks next to me. "We all came up in this game together." I continued. "We all survived some tough times in this game together. We all lost a few homies in this game together, and together we've made sure that they'll never ever be forgotten. We're family, and that's what family does for one another. That's why I took it upon myself to make sure when those cell doors close with me on the opposite side, the family will be well taken care of!" I said, causing Squirrel to smile.

"I want to be here, so I decided to leave someone I trust in my shoes. Don't get me wrong, I'll place my life in anyone of you niggas' hands, without a second guess. But, with position, comes power, and with power, comes envy. That's why I decided to place this person in position, because power isn't what they're after, and what man can ever be envious of a woman?"

Everyone in attendance looked at me as if I had the word *stupid* written all over my face. Before I said another word, Angel strutted out the back room looking like the boss bitch she was.

———

Angel

I LISTENED to Ken give his weak-ass-going-away speech. That's exactly why his members were betraying him. He wasn't the killa the streets once feared. The thought of prison made him soft. Although it was only Bull that jumped ship so far, I had no doubt, before the ship sunk, they'll all jump over. No one was ever willing to stick it out with the captain and go down with the ship.

Ken was giving a speech like this was the Super Bowl halftime show. I wasn't about to sit back and wait for him to introduce me like I was the halftime performer. I walked out the back room with all eyes on me. I could tell Squirrel was upset by the look he shot my way. Stupid ass, bald headed ass nigga thought that the throne was his. Ha! Fool ass nigga he was!

Ken stopped mid-sentence and smiled in my direction. I stood at the head of the table with him and looked around the room. All the men stared at me for two different reasons. Some stared at me with hate in their eyes, and the rest stared out of complete lust.

"Bruh, you got'ta be kidding me," Squirrel said, obviously disgusted by Ken's choice.

"What's the problem, Squirrel?" I asked him.

Squirrel's eyes shot at me like a set of bullets. "The problem is, you don't know shit about running B.M.B., and you ain't been here since day one, from the sandbox! You married yo' way into this shit!"

"And I guess you know how to run B.M.B." I toyed with him.

"I am B.M.B.!" he shot back.

"No, you're not! You're just a shadow!" I shot back at him with my own gun. I was tired of them thinking this was a man's world. A man's game.

"A shadow?" Squirrel said, like he didn't know what I was speaking of.

"Yes, a fuckin' shadow! That's all you've ever been in this game, a fuckin' shadow. Since I've been here, I haven't seen you put in any work. Who cares about what you've once did. For the past few years, all I've seen you do was: shout out orders and walk behind Ken, like his fuckin' shadow!"

"Bitch!" Squirrel flinched in my direction, but yes, he knew better. He looked at Ken and said, "So you're going to let her talk to me like that. After everything we've been through together?"

"I ain't saying shit, because it's best that y'all two get yo' differences behind y'all. This is the new B.M.B. She's taking my spot, and if you don't like it, there's the door!" Ken said. Even though he said it with authority, I knew it hurt him to let the words come out of his mouth.

Squirrel looked around the room. It seemed like everyone in the room had cement shoes. "So, y'all standing behind this—this bullshit!" Squirrel ranted. "A woman! One that ain't good for shit! Bruh, you met her in a strip club, and you married her. How the fuck you gon' try to turn a hoe into a housewife, then to a queenpin!" Squirrel shook his head in disgust. "You know what? I ain't fin'to let this bitch be the cause of me going down. Y'all got it. Don't call my phone when y'all got fed cases 'cause of this bitch!"

"I ain't gon' be too many more bitches!" I said.

"We'll see about that," Squirrel said just as he walked out the door and slammed it behind himself.

I looked at Ken. He looked as if he wanted to chase Squirrel. Bitch ass niggas made me sick. That's why I was taking over in the first place, 'cause neither of them deserved the got'damn throne! I cleared my throat to address the room.

"The door is there for anyone who wants to jump ship. Like Big Ken said, this is the new B.M.B. Since Ken's fed case has been going on, I've been the one in the trenches. I've been the one doing the drops. I've been in the traps seeing how hard you niggas been working. I noticed y'alls hustle, and it was me who brought it to Ken's attention to drop the price of every ki y'all buy by five hundred dollars. This is a team effort. That's what we are. A team. Nothing will change. I'll still be in the fields with y'all, and we'll help each other feed our families. B.M.B isn't a clique. We're a family. A tight-knit family. So, if we all consider each other family, it doesn't matter who cuts the turkey on Thanksgiving, or who eats at the head of the table, as long as we all get a plate, and a seat. The way Squirrel walked out on his family was a disgrace. Loyalty is a must. We don't turn our backs on each other for the throne. What we do is pull up another chair and we all sit together like family."

Everyone looked at me and nodded. Niggas didn't want to hear a speech about how they've been excellent workers. What they wanna hear is how they can make more money, with less sacrifices.

"With that being said, the door is open. But this will be your only chance to walk away without a bullet following behind you. And trust me, my guns bust too!" I assured them.

No one moved. I guess they did have cement on their shoes. I had won their loyalty. Now it was on to phase two. Send Ken away, forever!

16

ANGEL

The Next Day

Bull and I sat beside each other as we waited on the jury to finish deliberating on how long they were going to sentence Ken. The courtroom was so packed that people had to stand up in the back alongside the walls. Everyone wanted to see what was to come to the king of Dallas. Pistol and the entire B.M.B. family were in attendance. Jorge accompanied Lluvia's poncho wearing ass here. Surprisingly, Squirrel even showed his bald headed ass up. He didn't sit near our section; he just stood in the back by the door with all of the other groupies.

Even though Ken drove from home to the courthouse, once he entered the courthouse, he was placed in handcuffs so that he wouldn't put his hands on anyone else, specifically, Emmanuel. Ken had basically hanged himself by hitting his attorney, especially in front of the people who were about to determine his future.

As Emmanuel walked through the door, the crowd gasped. His eye had swelled up like a prune. A woman in the room looked at Emmanuel's eye, then she covered her mouth with her hand. I knew then that Ken's ass was through!

Emmanuel walked up beside a handcuffed Ken. Ken saw Emmanuel's eye and hung his head. I smiled on the inside. *That'll teach you to keep your fuckin' hands to yourself!*

The bailiff stood in front of the room and said, "All rise! The Honorable Judge Simpson." The audience stood as we waited for the judge to take her seat. "You may be seated," the bailiff said.

I smiled thinking how I was so glad that this will be our last time hearing that. Judge Simpson faced the jury. "Jury, I want you all to block out the incident that happened between Mr. Watson and his attorney. When you make your decision, make it based on the evidence that has been presented to the court. Also, keep in mind that the defendant changed his plea to *guilty*, and is asking for mercy from the court."

Yeah, right! Mercy my ass! Fry his ass all the way to hell, I thought to myself. The members of the jury nodded in unison. An elderly Caucasian lady stood with a small folded piece of paper. "We, the jury, deliberated long and hard on the sentencing phase. We have considered the amendment of guilt, and we've also considered the request for mercy, and leniency." The lady sighed then continued. "With that being said, we, the jury, request that Kendrick Watson be sentenced to five hundred and forty months on the counts of possession of a controlled substance weighing at four hundred and fifty-three grams, with the intent to distribute." The lady of the jury folded up the piece of paper and took her seat.

The audience went into a frenzy. Members of B.M.B. went into a yelling match with the jury. The bailiff had to call in for backup to get control of the courtroom. I heard the numbers that the jury sentenced Ken to, but math has never been my strong subject. A bitch can spell her ass off, but numbers, uh-uh!

I did the math in my head as best as I could. Twelve months in a year. Twenty-four months makes two years. Time it, carry the one. Oh shit! The jury had just sentenced Ken to forty-five years. Considering the federal court system classified thirty years as a life sentence, Ken was given life plus fifteen. I smiled. I finally got rid of his bitch ass!

———

Ken

WHEN THE JURY requested that I received five hundred and forty months, I nearly fainted. I didn't know how many years it was off the bat, but I knew anything past a hundred months was a long ass time. Once I did the math in my head, I couldn't do nothing but hang my head. It took everything in me not to cry. Forty-five years. *Forty-five fuckin' years!*

Who the fuck they think I killed? I was here for possession of cocaine, not murder. I knew, well, I thought maybe I would get maybe ten years max, especially the way the courts have been blessing those racist ass cops that's been killing black people left and right. I can recall a Dallas County judge sentencing a Caucasian woman who's a cop to ten years for going into another man's apartment and killing him in cold blood. Let's not forget the man was black, the cop was off duty, and a racist. But me, a hustler, I get a wam-bam-thank-you-ma'am! And the world screams justice! Justice for who?

I looked over to Emmanuel. He couldn't see me staring at him because the eye closest to me was closed shut. I can almost bet his uppity ass felt me staring at him. I swear, if looks could kill!

After the federal agents came in to assist the bailiff, the room fell silent. The judge looked at me and shook her head. I couldn't tell if she felt sorry for me or disgusted by me.

"Mr. Watson, I have to say, in all of my twenty years as a judge, I've never witnessed anyone in my courtroom ever punch their attorney." A few laughs came from the audience. "Your act of violence was displayed before the jury, so I can tell why they sentenced you to such a drastic number." As she talked, I hung my head. I had let my situation get the best of me. "I do have the final say-so in the sentencing phase. With that being said, I am sentencing you to three hundred and sixty months in a maximum federal facility. Would you like to say anything to the court on your behalf?" the judge asked.

I raised my head and said, "I would like to first apologize to my attorney for what I did, and I would like to apologize to my family, especially my wife for letting them down. If possible, I would like to request that I could have at least a week to get my affairs in order and say my goodbyes."

Judge Simpson looked at me, and for once I didn't see disgust, I saw pity. "I will grant you twenty-four hours from this hour to say your goodbyes. Tomorrow at nine o'clock I would like to see you turn yourself in. If you're even a minute late I will be sending U.S. Marshalls to find you, and your sentence will be extended!" She then banged her gavel and said, "Court is dismissed."

—————

Emmanuel

As Judge Simpson banged her gavel, Kendrick was sentenced to a forty-five-year sentence, and I was freed from his evil wife's web. Kendrick looked at me as I stuffed my papers in my suitcase. I was trying to get as far away from him as I possibly could. I told Janice to stay in the car. That way, once Kendrick was sentenced, we could leave and skip town. We were leaving town, and never looking back.

As the judge walked in her chamber, Kendrick's family and friends walked up to him and gave him their best wishes. I grabbed my suitcase and walked through the small swinging doors. I was stopped by Angel, or should I say, the devil!

"What do you want?" I asked her under my breath.

"I just want to say that I'm sorry for how things turned out," she said as she hid her smile well.

'*Yeah right*'! I thought to myself.

"Yeah, me too," I said as I tried to walk away, but she stepped in my path.

"I'll be in touch," she said as she stepped to the side.

As I walked to the door, a man with a bald head, and a gold mouth full of gold stepped into my way. "I see you and Angel are pretty close," the man with golds said.

"I don't know what you're talking about."

The man with gold teeth grilled me. The look he gave me sent chills down my spine. "I'll be watching you," he said as he moved to the side to let me pass.

As soon as I walked in the hallway, I dialed Janice's number. "Yes!" she said, answering on the first ring.

"I'm on my way out," I spoke softly into the phone.

"What happened?" she asked. I could hear the car crank up in the background.

I sighed and said, "He got fucked over."

17

ANGEL

Later That Night

The club was packed to capacity. People were still waiting outside in a line that circled around the block. Everyone in the city tried to attend Big Ken's going away party. The flyers should've said, 'Big Ken's funeral', because after tonight Ken would be dead to the world.

Everyone who was someone was here to celebrate with us. The entire Bloody Money Bag family was here. Pistol, and a few of Ken's old high school friends. Jas' stayed in the city for yet another night. She claimed it was to support me. Bitch, please! I knew it was so that she could stay close to Smurf. I didn't know if they had started fucking or not, but Jas' was most def' sprung off of something Smurf was feeding her big booty ass.

I was a little upset that Chelsea couldn't make it. Her husband had her on a tight leash. He damn near reported her AWOL the last time she came out to the club with us.

That's what her ass gets for marrying a marine. While her light-skinned ass is stuck in the house, I'll be in my big ass house by myself, with a smile so big Ken would be able to see it all the way from his new prison cell.

I paid the DJ to play Big Ken's favorite song. I waited for the song to start before I signaled the bottle girls to surprise Ken with his favorite champagne, *Ace of Spades*. Meek Millz came over the speaker.

AIN'T this what they've been waitin' for? / You ready? Uh, uh / I used to pray for times like this, to rhyme like this / So I had to grind like that to shine like this / In a matter of time I spent on some locked-up shit / In the back of a paddy wagon, cuffs locked on wrist / Seen my dreams unfold, nightmares come true / It was time to marry the game and I said, "Yeah, I do." / If you want it, you gotta see it with a clear-eyed view / Got a shorty, she tryna bless me like I said achoo / Like a nigga sneezed, nigga please, 'fore them triggers squeeze / I'm gettin' cream, never let them hoes get in between—

THE BOTTLES with sparkles lit up the night life. The bottles came from all angles, right up to Ken as he stood posted up in the VIP area. I could see that Ken wasn't in the party mood. Hell, I wouldn't be either. I'm lying. If this was my last night free, I would've made sure I went away with a bunch of memories.

I grabbed a bottle of *Ace of Spades* from the metal tray and handed the gold bottle to Ken. He accepted the bottle, but not happily. "Babe, smile for me, please. Don't let our last night end like this. Trust me, I'm going to be by your side, for however long you stay in there. I swear!" I said as I kissed his cheek.

Ken took the bottle to the head as he tried to drink away his sorrows, his regrets. "You hear that, babe? That's yo' song they're playing." I smiled at him. "I did that. Just for you, daddy." Ken smiled and pulled me into his arms. I rested my ass on his midsection as Meek rapped Ken's favorite part.

And I'm the king of my city 'cause I'm still callin' them shots /And these lames talkin' that bullshit the same niggas that flock / I'm the same nigga from Berks Street with them nappy braids that lock / The same nigga that came up and I had to wait for my spot / And these niggas hatin' on me, hoes waitin' on me / Still on that hood shit, my Rolls-Royce on E / They gon' remember me, I say remember me / So much money have yo' friends turn in yo' enemies / And when there's beef I turn my enemies to memories / With them bricks they go for 40, ain't no 10 a key / Hold up, broke nigga turn rich, love the game like Mitch / And if I leave, you think them pretty hoes gon' still suck my dick? / It was somethin' about that Rollie when it first touched my wrist / Had me feelin' like that dope boy when he first touched that brick
 I'm gone

I LAUGHED to myself and thought, *Literally!*

———

Ken

I MOUTHED the words to my favorite song, *Dreams &
Nightmares*. It was crazy how the two coincided. One day
I'm living out my dream. I'm talkin' 'bout pallets of kilos
at my disposal, shooters ready to kill at my beck and call. I
governed a solid team that I knew I could trust with my
life. I had the flyest whips in the city, and let's not discuss
hoes. I only had one, but hands down, she was the baddest
in the city.

I kissed Angel's head as she danced in my embrace.
Her lil short ass felt good in my arms. She didn't know it,
but I was gon' fuck her brains out until nine o'clock in the
morning. Shid, I might even make the US Marshals come
and get me out the pussy.

The DJ came over the loudspeaker. "Ladies and gentlemen, we are here to celebrate tonight for one reason, and
one reason only. We're here to salute the big homie, Big
Ken, as he travels like a gangsta upstate." The crowd went
berserk.

"Bloody Money Bag is in the building!" DJ Spillz
shouted. My squad raised their bottles to the ceiling. "We
got bad bitches in the building!" Angel screamed as DJ
Spillz spoke. "This is all for the real, the one and only big,
big homie. This is for you, Big Ken. We salute you!" DJ
Spillz gave me a proper farewell.

Everyone looked at me and started clapping. This was
my city. Dallas was my home, my stomping grounds. This
was my family. And I was going to miss them dearly. All of
them.

I looked to the stage as an overhead projector turned on

and a screen started coming down from the ceiling. "What's this?" I asked Angel as I pointed to the screen.

"A lil som' something," Angel said, sounding like Cardi B. A bottle girl walked over and handed Angel a microphone. I looked at my wife, wondering what the hell she had up her sleeve.

Angel touched the head of the microphone with the palm of her hand. "Attention, everyone!" she shouted. "As you all know, the bitch ass feds are sending my man away. They can take Big Ken away from us, but they can't take away the memories we all shared with him. With that being said, I would like to direct everyone's attention to the screen."

I looked at the screen as images of me and my team popped up on the screen. I couldn't do nothing but laugh. As the images changed, the more the realization hit me that I was actually going to prison, and for a very long time. Images of me and Angel at our wedding popped up. We were fly as hell. We wanted to prove to everyone that we were different, so we didn't wear the normal black tux and white gown. At our wedding, I rocked a red and black Louis V' tux, and Angel rocked a red Dolce & Gabbana gown. You couldn't tell either of us shit that day. That was a day I would never forget.

The slideshow changed again. This time, the picture was one of me and Squirrel. I shook my head and looked up to the ceiling to hold back the tears. Damn, I really missed my guy. Angel must've felt my pain, because she hugged me.

The next picture was of me and uncle Turtle. I almost cried looking at the picture. It was a picture of me and Unc' when I was a teenager. I can still remember the conversation we were having at that exact moment. I swear it didn't feel right spending my last hours of freedom without him. I hate that I let the feds scare me away from seeing him.

The screen suddenly went black, then the power cut off in the whole club. As fast as the lights went out, the quicker they came back on. Instead of pictures being on the screen, it looked as if it had been changed to a video of some kind. There was a man sitting in a chair, with some kind of bag over his head.

"Angel, what is this?" I asked.

Angel shrugged and said, "I don't know. I never seen that before."

A voice over the video said, "Can they hear me?"

Someone else answered, "Clear as day."

A figure walked in front of the camera with a blue ski mask on. He adjusted the camera so that the person that was sitting down could be seen with him.

"Big Ken!" the masked man said. "Or should I say, little Ken! Guess who!"

18

BISHOP

"Sit his bitch ass up!" I ordered my shooter—Snake. Snake got his nickname by the way he talked. After every word he spoke, it sounded like he was hissing. Snake wasn't born that way. When he went to prison, he was in a riot against the Tango Blast. One of the Hispanic gang members cut his throat, clipping his vocal cord. Ever since the incident, Snake walked around with a hiss in his voice that turned out to be his trademark.

Snake wrestled with a tied up Turtle as he tried to sit him up in the wooden chair. I laughed as I watched Turtle squirm for his life. There was a bag over his head, so he couldn't see our faces. I didn't really care if he did. I wasn't letting Turtle live past the night unless Ken followed through on my request.

As Snake fought to get Turtle's old ass in the seat, I looked at the computer wiz, who was my cousin—Freak. "How's it going, Freak?" I asked him as he typed some codes on his computer.

I patted Freak on his shoulder. "Make it happen, and watch yo' cousin do the rest."

I walked towards Turtle who was finally sitting in the wooden chair that sat in the center of the room. There were two bright lights on both sides of him. A camcorder was posted in front of him on a stand, ready to record. I snatched the bag off of Turtle's head. His nose was bleeding, and his eyes were black. Turtle looked at me and asked, "Who are you, and what do you want?"

I pulled the ski mask from off my face and stared at Turtle. I squatted down to his eye level. Even though he shared the same blood as Ken bitch ass, I still respected him as an OG in the game, to a certain extent.

"My name is Bishop. You probably don't know me, only because I'm not an attention seeker. I do my dirt under the radar. But, I do want you to know that this shit," I said, waving my hand around the room. "This shit between me and you, it's not personal."

"Then what the hell is it then, because I damn sho'll don't know you."

"You're right, Turtle. You don't know me. But, your nephew, Ken does. Your nephew killed my baby brother. His name was Knight. My little brother was all that I had. I loved him more like a son than a brother. Your nephew took him away from me. He took the closest thing to my heart."

"I'm sorry about your brother. But, however, the situation with your brother and my nephew, that is between the two of them. When you take it upon yo'self to avenge your brother's death, then that makes it personal!" Turtle said.

I thought about what the old head said.

"I did it! I tap'd into the club's security system!"

"Excuse me, old head," I politely said as I excused myself and walked over to Freak. "Did you find Ken?" I asked Freak as I looked at all the security cameras in the club.

Freak nodded and said with a smile, "He's right there."

I looked closer. "Can you zoom in?"

Freak typed on his keyboard; the security footage grew larger on the screen. I looked at Ken and smiled. "Snake, Country!" I shouted, calling after my most trusted soldiers. "Get the old head ready. It's showtime!"

Angel

EVERYONE in the club looked at the screen in horror. I looked at Ken; his jaws were locked. His face showed nothing but anger. At first, I couldn't tell who was hiding behind the ski mask, until the masked man stepped back from the camera and said, "Big Ken! Or should I say, little Ken. Guess who?"

A man sat in a chair with something over his face. I already knew who was behind unlucky door number one. Turtle! I couldn't expose the surprise to Ken by telling him, so I had to wait and seem shocked like everyone else would be once they saw Turtle's face.

Ken walked closer to the screen. "Ken, can you see me? Can you hear me?" Bishop asked.

Ken nodded, not sure if Bishop could hear him, then he said, "Yeah, I can hear you."

Bishop smiled from behind the ski mask. "You sound different fam'. You sound . . . scared."

"Who are you, and what do you want?" Ken asked.

"You know exactly who I am. You have to know, I mean, you did kill my lil brother!" Bishop shouted.

"Bishop!" Ken shouted. He looked surprised.

"Well, now, that would be dry-snitching, huh. Screaming my name like that in front of everyone," Bishop said, laughing. "I guess I don't need this anymore," he said as pulled the ski mask off of his face and tossed it to the ground.

"Damn, Bishop, you still on that shit? That shit was over a year ago, homie!" Ken shouted in disbelief.

"A year! What? I'm supposed to forget you off'd my brother, just because a lil time then passed! The fuck wrong with you!" Bishop managed to laugh through all of his anger. "I'm not really on that any more though." He laughed again, then said. "I'm on this!" Bishop snatched the sheet from off of Turtle's head.

Those of them in the audience that knew Turtle gasped in shock. I looked around for Bull, then I remembered that I had sent him off on another mission. Ken looked at Pistol, Pistol walked beside Ken and I heard Ken whisper something to Pistol that I couldn't quite make out. Pistol pulled out his phone and made a phone call. Pistol pulled his phone from his ear and looked at the screen.

"Don't waste yo' time—all the phone signals are jammed," Bishop said with a weird laugh.

"Unc', are you okay?" Ken said to Turtle.

"I'm good, nephew," Turtle replied.

"He's good right now," Bishop said. "But, if you don't

get me what I want, you'll be burying him like I buried my brother."

"What is it that you want?" Ken asked curiously.

"What you think yo' uncle is worth, huh?" Bishop taunted.

"The world, and everything in it!" Ken said. I looked at the back of Ken's head, wondering if he would say the same thing about me if it was my ass in that chair tied up.

"As much as a man desires everything in the world, I'll settle for something a little simpler."

"Like?" Ken asked.

"Two hundred ki's."

19

KEN

I called in every favor that was owed to me to get the product that Bishop had requested in exchange for my uncle's life. I knew I had a little over twenty ki' in the safe at the stash house. Out of all the ki's Luis shot to Angel, she only had fifty left. The deal she made with the team to drop the price down five hunnit a ki' hurt more than it helped. The squad all together bought fifty ki's together that night. I was glad to see them dedicated to what Angel was trying to do, but now that I needed the ki's I didn't have them.

I pulled up to Luis' house with Angel in the passenger seat. Luis was expecting me, so the front gate was already open. This was the first time I've been to Luis' house at this time of the morning. The grass still had its morning dew on it. I made Luis my last option. I didn't want to go to him unless I had no other choice. And I had no other choice.

Jorge and Filipe met me at the front door. "I'm sorry to hear about your uncle, Ken," Filipe said.

I shook their hands. "Me too, Ken. Your uncle was a good man!" Jorge said.

I nodded. I was at a loss for words. I never in a million years thought I would be in this predicament. Angel stood behind me quietly as well. I couldn't tell what was on her mind, but whatever it was, she kept it to herself.

Filipe and Jorge escorted us inside. Luis was waiting for us on the couch in his Italian silk house robe. As I walked in the room, Lluvia ran into my arms, tears were falling down her cheek one after the other. Angel crossed her arms with an apparent attitude. At this point, I didn't give two fucks. I wasn't in the mood for her shit right now, and I think she got the point.

"I'm sorry to hear about Turtle. When my father told me that he had been kidnapped, it brought back horrible memories when I was kidnapped by my father's enemies. God only knows how they are treating him." Lluvia cried.

Luis stood up to embrace me. "Whatever you need, I'm here to help," he said.

"Thank you, Luis." I sighed then said, "I do need a huge favor." I sat down. Angel stood up beside me like she was my bodyguard.

"Anything you need, just name it," Luis said as he placed his hands together.

"I need you to sell me another fifty ki's, and front me fifty more. The kidnappers demanded two hundred ki's in exchange for Turtle. I have a hundred, I just need to come up with the other half they want."

Luis nodded and said, "I don't have it handy, but I can have it to you in the next say . . . three to four hours."

"Thank you, Luis. And, I promise I'll pay you back, with interest."

"It's okay. I know if the shoe was on the other foot, Turtle would do the same for me. Is there anything else I can help you with?" Luis asked.

"Guns, something to go to war with," I said.

"You have soldiers, right?" Luis asked.

"You can never have too many," I said as I looked at Luis. Luis nodded and then he looked at Filipe.

"What should I prepare the soldiers for?" Filipe said.

I looked at Filipe and said, "Prepare them for war!"

———

Bull

I SAT OUTSIDE of Ken's lawyer's house. Angel had me on another mission after failing the first one. This was my chance to prove myself to her again. This one was going to be like taking candy from a baby. All I had to do was kill Emmanuel and his assistant. Angel insisted that I make it look like a hit that came from Ken. Angel was smart as hell in my book, dangerously smart. She was trying to tie up loose ends while solidifying Ken would never see daylight ever again.

Angel had accomplished her mission. She played a heavy hand in getting Ken sentenced to thirty years in a federal prison. Not only that, but Ken's dumb, pussy-whipped ass made Angel the new head of B.M.B. Little did he know, he had handed her everything she wanted on a silver—no, fuck that, a gold platter. I don't care what people think of me, I had to get a piece of Angel's hot pussy. Whatever she had between her thighs had Big Ken's head fucked up.

I killed the engine and emptied my pockets, placing everything in the middle console. I checked the clip on my fo-five, I clicked the safety off and tucked my heat on my waist. I opened the car door, then hesitated. A delivery man was walking up to Emmanuel's front door. I thought about using the delivery man as a way to get inside, but I quickly dismissed the thought. Using the delivery man would mean that I would have to off him too. I didn't want any unnecessary casualties.

I sat back and waited for the delivery man to make his delivery. Once he was done, I was going to slide in and take care of my business unseen, then dip off just as fast. I was semi in my feelings because I was missing what was to be the party of the year, Ken's going-away-forever party.

Emmanuel's front door opened. I watched closely as Emmanuel said something to the delivery man. The next thing I saw, the food that the delivery man was holding fell to the ground, then the delivery man pulled out a gun and aimed it directly in Emmanuel's face.

I shook my head and thought, '*Not again!*'

20

EMMANUEL

"Grab another suitcase for me, babe," I said to Janice as we rushed to pack all of our important things so we could leave town.

I grabbed my bar exam certification, my high school diploma, and my college diploma. I had already filled up two suitcases with nothing but clothes. Before we came to my house, we stopped at Janice's apartment to grab some of her things, then we came here. I felt for some odd reason that we were on borrowed time. When Angel said that she would be in touch, I felt that she was giving me a fair warning, a threat—no, a promise. But when Kendrick requested that he spend his last hours with his family, I also felt that he had a hidden agenda.

"Here, babe, this is the last one," Janice said as she dragged the suitcase and laid it in front of me.

She sat on the floor and crossed her legs, Indian-style. "Are you okay?" I asked. "You don't have to go with me if you don't want to."

She looked at me and said, "I'm fine, I promise." She crawled on her knees to me and said, "I will follow you all over the earth if that's what you want me to do." She looked deeply into my eyes. I could feel her truth through her eyes. "I love you, Manny."

It had been a while since I last told a woman I loved her. I love my wife, Hannah. With work and my busy schedule, I rarely even told her how I felt, or even showed her for that matter. When Hannah cheated on me, I never imagined I would love again. God knows I wasn't searching for it. And I did my best to hide from it in every way. That was until the night Janice showed me her true colors. I had always thought that Janice was very attractive. Before that day, I never looked at Janice more than just a co-worker. Now she was more. She wasn't just a co-worker. She was more than just a friend. She was my lover.

Over the past few weeks, Janice has shown me that it's safe. That a man can get injured in the game, sit on the bench and recover, and have the courage to get back in the game to give it another shot. I cared for Janice deeply. I was only holding back because I was thinking about both of us. I couldn't afford another heartbreak, and I didn't want to cause her one either. But I had to be honest with her, I figured I owed her that much.

"I love you too, Janice," I said, exposing my true feelings. Janice let her tears fall down her cheeks as she leaned over the suitcase to kiss me.

As our lips found each other, the doorbell rang. Janice jumped back and looked at me with fear in her eyes. I jumped up and grabbed my gun that was in the drawer of the nightstand.

"Stay behind me," I whispered to Janice. I led the way down the stairs, gun in hand, aimed at the front of me like they taught at the gun range.

"Who is it!" I yelled as I stood in front of the door. Janice hid from behind me like a scared little girl. She practically was using me as a shield.

"*DoorDash*!" A male voice boomed from the other side of the door.

I peeped through the peephole. A man stood on the other side of the door with a *DoorDash* hat on. He held a plastic sack with food inside.

I looked back at Janice and laughed. "It's just a delivery man."

I unlocked the door and opened it. "*DoorDash*, sir," the man said. I couldn't see his face because his hat was pulled down too far.

"I'm sorry, you must've got the wrong address, because we didn't order anything."

The delivery man looked up at me. I stared at him as I tried to remember where I knew his face from. He smiled as he dropped the sack of food. His gold plated teeth reminded me of where I knew him from, but then it was too late. His gun was already in my face.

Ken

THE TIME WAS 8:45 a.m. I was due to turn myself in at nine on the dot. I wasn't going to make it one time; the judge was just going to have to send the marshals to get me. I wasn't turning myself in without getting my uncle back first.

I sat on the couch and stared at my iPhone that was on the coffee table in front of me. Smurf, Pistol, and my wife Angel stood in the room as we all waited for my phone to ring. No one had anything to say as we all waited in silence. My mind was all over the place, so I could only tell where theirs were. Luis had come through for me with the ki's. I gathered up the ki's that were left over from the first shipment. Luis had sent me ten shooters to watch my back when we finally did the transaction.

Angel was the first to break the awkward silence. "Why won't he call already, ughhh!" she shouted in frustration.

I placed both of my hands on the side of my head. I was past frustrated. I was itching to kill someone. If Bishop even laid a hand on my uncle, I was going to body the rest of Bishop's family like I did his little brother, Knight.

My phone started ringing. We all jumped and just stared at the phone. "Answer it!" Angel yelled, snapping me back to reality.

My mind was in a daze. I experienced the same feeling when Lluvia got kidnapped by her father's enemies. I was always used to being in control, but the kidnappers always made me feel vulnerable. Like I was at their will. And I was.

"Hello!" I said into the phone as I placed the call on speaker.

"I hope you got what I asked for, 'cause you out of time!" Bishop said, like he didn't have a care in the world. His careless demeanor made me want to kill him even more. He was in control, and he knew it. It was all a part of the game. Supply and demand.

"Yeah, I got it. I was just waiting on you to call. Just tell me where you wanna meet up at?" I was ready to get this whole thing over with. I wanted to get my uncle back safely and turn myself in.

"Tonight, at Mondo's tire shop off of Harry Hines," Bishop instructed.

"Wait!" I shouted. "Why later tonight? Why not right now? I have to turn myself in any minute now. Before I do that, I have to make sure everything with the exchange is on the up and up!" I explained.

"What you tellin' me all that bullshit for! I didn't wanna see yo' face anyway." Bishop laughed, then said, "Oh, you thought I wanted you to make the delivery?" He laughed again.

"If not me, then who?" I asked, curiously.

"Your fine ass wife!"

———

Angel

I KNOW this nigga didn't! I just know he didn't. I looked around the room hoping I was the only one that heard that motherfucka say my name. "What did he just say?" I asked, hoping I'd heard wrong.

"Oh! She's there right now?" Bishop asked excitedly. "Can she hear me?" he asked.

Ken looked at me. His pain was clear as day in his eyes. "Yes, she can hear you," Ken said.

"Sweetheart, what's your name?" Bishop asked me.

I looked at Ken for permission; he nodded. "Angel," I replied.

"Indeed you are," Bishop said. "Angel babe, do you want to help your husband get his uncle back?" Bishop asked me.

"Of course!" I replied. But on the inside I was screaming, *fuck that nigga!*

"Well, since you want to see him home safely, you need to deliver the ki's to me, by yourself!" Bishop demanded.

Ken snatched up the phone and said, "Come on, Bishop! Don't put my wife in this shit, fam'." Ken sighed and said, "I'll come by myself if that's what you want."

"Nah, you just turn yo'self in, homie. If it ain't wifey alone, then it ain't nobody." The line went silent, then Bishop said, "Angel darling."

"Yes?" I answered

"Don't be late!" Bishop said as he hung up, leaving us to listen to the dial tone.

Ken threw his phone at the wall as hard as he could. "He's going to kill unc'," Ken said, just above a whisper.

I hugged him tight and said, "No, he's not. You wanna know why?" Ken didn't answer. "Because I'm going to take the ki's to him like he asked."

Ken broke away from me and said, "No, the fuck you ain't!" he shouted as he stared directly into my eyes. "Bishop hates me. You delivering the ki's will be right up his alley. That means he'll have you and Unc'. If there's any way he could make me miserable, it would be to take away the two people I love the most."

As soon as Ken finished talking, the hinges to the front

door flew off; the U.S. Marshals stormed inside like they were a part of the S.W.A.T team.

"Kendrick Watson, get on the ground, now!"

Ken dropped down to his knees and placed his hands behind his head. He was cuffed and brought to his feet. Ken looked into my eyes and said, "Angel, please!"

The Marshals held Ken's arms as he held his gaze on me. "Babe, just trust me, I got this. Remember, I was taught by the best," I said, convincing, or at least I hoped I was. The Marshals let me give Ken one kiss, a peck really. As they pulled his arm, forcing him to leave, Ken yelled over his shoulder to Pistol, "P, take care of my wife!" Pistol nodded as the Marshals shoved Ken out the hole in the wall that used to be our front door.

As we watched Ken get escorted to a black Yukon we all stood in silence, until Smurf said, "Queen, what's the plan?"

I clenched my teeth to hold my laughter in. Everything I had planned had worked out, or was working out, so to say. The only problem was Bishop. He had thrown a huge wrench in the game. He caught me off guard, and now it was my turn to return the favor.

I looked at Smurf and said, "Show them who Blood Money Bag really are!"

21

EMMANUEL

Janice stood frozen as the delivery man held his gun in my face. "Don't make any sudden moves, or I'll empty the whole clip in you, and pistol-whoop that pretty lil snow bunny behind you."

I took slow, steady steps backwards, careful so I wouldn't force the gunman's hands. I held my hands up, exactly where he could see them as he stepped inside and closed the door behind himself. "Get over there, take a seat with him!" he demanded of Janice.

As I sat down slowly, Janice sat right beside me, like in a way, under me. I knew she was scared, hell, I was too. Janice began to cry. I knew in her mind she thought for sure we were about to die. In a sense, I felt the same way. The gunman held his gun at us, Janice was baby crying by now all in my ear. She pulled her knees to her chest and let it rip. I knew she was scared, but now I knew the meaning of being scared shitless.

"Bitch, if you don't shut . . . the fuck . . . up!" the gunman yelled in frustration.

Janice's tears stopped instantly. And I was glad too. In every movie that I had seen with situations like this, crying always gets them killed faster, and I wasn't in no rush to die. "Do you know who I am?" the gunman asked.

"You're the man from the courtroom, right?" I was already sure he was the same man, but I was doing my best to stall. That was another thing I saw in movies in situations like this, stalling gives people an opportunity to find some way out.

The gunman nodded. "You can call me Squirrel, if you like. I'm here on behalf of Big Ken, or as you'd say, Kendrick."

And there it was. Another thing I remember from the movies. Squirrel giving his name only meant one thing, and one thing only. We were good as dead. Rest in peace to us. I can already see my tombstone: *Here lies a noble dead nigga!*

But something he said caught me completely off guard. "Big Ken?"

"Don't start playing stupid with me, lawyer boy. You got a college degree, don't waste it," he said as he kept his gun aimed at me.

"Kendrick sent you, why?" I asked, curiously. I couldn't help but wonder if Kendrick had found out about what me and Angel did. About the deal I made with her, the deal I was forced into taking.

"He wants to know why you fucked him over. He wants to know if the feds forced you to throw the case."

I knew we were about to die. It was evident in why he

exposed his name, and why he was here. I had seen it in the movies countless amounts of time, but this wasn't the movies; this was real fucking life, our lives. And they were dangling by a thread, a thin one at that. I felt bad that I had dragged Janice into my mess. A mess that I didn't make myself, but it was still a mess I should've cleaned up before I invited company over, no matter who made it. Janice deserved better. Kendrick deserved better. He deserved the truth, even if it killed me. Even if he still had to spend the rest of his life in prison.

"It wasn't the feds," I said.

"Then who was it?" Squirrel asked as he sat on the edge of his seat like what I was about to say would change the world.

"It was—" I managed to say, but the doorbell caused me to stop.

Squirrel looked at me with his gun aimed at my head. "You expecting company?" he asked under his breath.

I thought about screaming. I wanted to, badly, but either way I knew it would only cause me to die faster. And I still wasn't quite ready to die. So, I shook my head and said, "No, but I also wasn't expecting you either." The doorbell rang twice more.

"Get up!" Squirrel demanded. Janice and I both jumped to our feet. "Lawyer boy, answer the door!" he demanded as he pointed his gun at the back of Janice's head. He was letting me know, one wrong move, and she was dead. "Snow bunny, you better not make any sudden moves, or I promise," he said without finishing his threat, but we got the picture.

I stood in front of the door and silently prayed that the

police would be on the other side once I opened it. Sharp shooters with expertise skills in getting people out of situations as this one. "Who is it!" I said with my fingers crossed.

"It's Hannah!"

I stood frozen in place. Janice looked at me as if Squirrel wasn't even behind her with a gun in his hand as she placed her hands on her hips. I shrugged and said, "Go away! I don't want to talk to you!" I shouted through the door. I silently prayed, 'Lord, please let her tramp ass just walk away.'

Squirrel placed his gun to the back of my head and whispered, "Open the door, slowly."

I shook my head. "Just let her go. She'll leave, I promise."

Squirrel snatched Janice up by her arm roughly. He placed his gun at her temple and said, "Open it!" I sighed. I had no other choice. I mean, why would I swap out a dime for a penny. I unlocked the door and slowly pulled it open. Hannah began to talk as soon as I pulled the door open.

"Manny, I'm sorry! Please forgive me, I'm preg—" She froze mid-sentence when she saw the gun in Squirrel's hand aimed at Janice's head.

"Manny, what's going on?" Hannah asked. I don't know why she asked me; hell, I wasn't the one holding the damn gun.

Janice back-kicked Squirrel in the balls, and the gun went off in the roof as Squirrel hunched over in pain. "Run!" I yelled as we all took off out the front door.

Our escape was cut short as Hannah ran directly into

another gunman. "Uhhhhhhhh! Where you think you going?" the second gunman said sarcastically.

Squirrel walked out the front door, clutching his man parts. He shoved his gun at the back of my head. "Bull, what the fuck are you doing here?" Squirrel asked the second gunman.

Bull laughed like the situation was hilarious. "I'm saving yo' ass, that's that I'm doing."

Ken

I STRIPPED out of my clothes until I was completely naked. The male officer made me hold my nuts so that he could look under them, then he made me spread my cheeks. The whole process was degrading. I couldn't figure out what kind of man wakes up every day to clock in to see another man's genitals. I guess that's the true meaning of *each its own*. I was glad he didn't make me squat and cough like they do in the movies.

The officer that searched me handed me an orange two-piece top and bottom. After I finished dressing, I was escorted to a dorm. Each dorm had its own cell block, and each cell block had its own cells. I was escorted to a cell with four bunks in it. I placed my thin mattress on the top bunk, which was the only available bunk in the cell. There were already three other people in the cell, two Blacks, and one Hispanic man. The Hispanic man slept across from me on the opposite top bunk. The bunks were so close, I could stick my arms out and I'll be able to touch the other bunk.

The two black cellies were drinking coffee, one of them looked at me and asked, "What's yo' name, homie?" The man was tall and skinny. Before I could answer him, he said: "They call me Slim. I could see why they called him Slim. The man was barely holding up the clothes he had on.

"You can call me Big Ken," I replied.

"Big Ken? The . . . Big Ken . . . from Dallas?" Slim asked, sounding like he had heard of me.

"Yeah, you know me or something?" I asked. I was more concerned than I should've been, but then again you never know who your enemies are when you have your own team that creates problems that you know nothing about.

"Not personally, I don't. But, I've heard nothing but real shit about you, and the movement you put together in Dallas." He stopped and then laughed as if he had just thought of something. "Did you really punch yo' lawyer in the courtroom with the jury present?" Slim asked.

I laughed too as I thought back to the stupid shit I had done that ruined my chances of a lighter sentence. It wasn't funny at all at the time, but now that I think about it, it was pretty insane. "Yeah, I did punch my lawyer. I was pissed. But, that shit hurt me more than it hurt him in the long run!" I explained. Thinking back, I never got a chance to apologize to Emmanuel for what I did. What I did was wrong, and in the game I'm in, it wasn't gangsta. Every kingpin that's ever got sentenced to any time, they hold their heads up high, and let nothing steal their shine. I let my emotions steal my shine.

Slim nodded as he finally stopped laughing at me.

"Well, Big Ken, if there's anything you need, just let me know."

I looked at the gray phones that lined the walls outside the cells. "What time do they let us use the phone?" I asked.

"You don't want to use them phones; they record every word we say," Slim explained. "If you don't mind me asking, how much time did they give you?"

"Thirty years," I said.

"Ouch!" Slim shouted like my years hurt him. Slim looked over his shoulders to make sure no one was coming. "You won't be here long, they'll probably have you on a plane by sunrise. Mansfield is just a transit unit. Here," Slim said as he pulled out a vintage flip phone. "Reach out to yo' people, I'll watch out for you."

I stared at the phone. It had been almost fifteen years since I last used a flip phone. I didn't think they still made them. Thank God they did. I instantly dialed Angel's number; it went straight to voicemail. I redialed her number, and got the same results. Aggravated, I dialed Pistol's number; he picked up on the first ring.

"Pistol!" I yelled into the phone a little too loud. Slim looked at me like I was tripping. Little did Slim know what my team was about to do at this exact moment.

"What's good? Who's this?" Pistol said into the phone.

"Ken, fool!" I said, but not as loud.

"Oh shit, family, you good?"

"Fuck how I'm doing. How's Angel?" I asked, concerned.

"Angel . . . she's making the run as we speak."

22

ANGEL

"What's love got to do, got to do with it? What's love, but a second-hand emotion? What's love got to do, got to do with it? Who needs a heart, when a heart can be broken!" I sung my heart out as loud as I possibly could to Tina Turner's song, *What's Love Got to Do with It*.

I was driving a rented U-Haul to meet up with Bishop to exchange the two hundred kilos for Turtle. At first, I can honestly say that I was scared to meet up with Bishop by myself. That was until I put a plan together in my head that would change the game for good. I had told my sister Chels' about what I had to do, and her messy ass told her husband Trent. Being that Trent had a military background, he decided to meet up with me and give me some pointers on how to survive. Lord knows I could use it.

I sat parked in an isolated parking lot as I waited for Trent's red Monte Carlo to pull up. As I was waiting, a set of headlights flashed in the abandoned parking lot. I turned the key and pulled alongside the Monte Carlo. I stepped out of the U-Haul with a big cheesy smile. It was showtime.

———

THERE WAS NO MUSIC PLAYING, no sounds but the old Monte Carlo's engine as I pulled up to the address Bishop had given me. I looked up at the roof and noticed two men up there with automatic rifles. Bishop was prepared for an ambush. Someone whistled, and then the garage door began to open. The lights were on, and the garage was full of Bishop's soldiers. As I pulled in, I noticed Turtle sittin' in a wooden chair, his hands tied behind his back. A sheet was over his face, preventing him from seeing anything.

I killed the engine as I parked. I sat still for a brief second so that I could peep the scene. I looked around for every possible exit, just like Trent had explained to me. As I saw what I thought was an exit, Bishop walked out the room with a huge grin on his face. I stepped out of the car and closed the door. Bishop walked up to me with his arms stretched out like we were old pals.

"Let's get down to business. I still have a hair appointment I'm trying to keep!" I said, getting straight to business.

Bishop laughed. "Ken taught you well, I see. Straight to business." He walked up to me, looking me up and down, then he circled around me. "I really can't believe Ken let you come by yo'self. But then again, I heard the feds kicked his door down this morning dragging him out the house. So, I guess he didn't really have any other choices. I guess it's only fair to sacrifice the queen in order to protect the king, huh?"

I shook my head, "What is with you and all these chess names and stories. I just don't get it."

"Well, get this, if you didn't come with all two hundred ki's, I'm killing Turtle, and I'm going to let my guys have their way with you, then I'ma kill you on Instagram live. Make you a star, a super star!" Bishop said.

"You know, I figured you would say something like that," I said as I now walked around Bishop like I owned the place. His goons stared at my ass as I walked around. "See, it's only five ki's in the car, but don't worry, I got the rest close by," I said, then laughed.

"You think this is funny! I wasn't playing when I said to come alone!" Bishop threatened.

"Bishop, Bishop, Bishop. You had to know I wasn't going to come alone with two hundred ki's. So if you want to kill me go right ahead, but that U-Haul right across the street is going to pull off, and your hopes of being the next head nigga in charge will be driving away with it. So, if you'll excuse me, I need to check on what I came for!" I said as I brushed past Bishop to get to Turtle.

Bishop looked at his goons that were posted by the door and said, "Raise the door, let me see the U-Haul this bitch is talking about."

I walked up to Turtle and yanked the sheet from over his head. The bright lights blinded him as he instantly hung his head until they finally adjusted.

"Angel, where is Kendrick?" Turtle asked.

"He's away, forever. I'm here now, and he left me in charge," I said as the garage door slowly opened.

"Forever?" Turtle asked, curiously. "What do you mean *forever?*"

"Ken was sentenced to thirty years, so he's never coming home. And you know what, Turtle, I'm so happy he won't ever be coming home."

My words caught the whole room by surprise, especially Turtle. "What are you saying, Angel?" Turtle asked.

"You know what the fuck I'm saying. Yo' bitch ass nephew got what the fuck he deserved," I said.

"Got what he deserved? You disloyal bitch! He gave you everything you ever asked for and more!" Turtle was pissed; it was written all over his face. He no longer cared or even thought of him being tied to a chair. He was channeling all his anger in on me.

"You're right. He did give me everything I wanted, and so much more. What about the shit he gave me I never asked for, huh! Huh!" I shouted in Turtle's face.

"What the fuck are you talkin' about, Angel? That man gave you the world."

"No, that man gave me black eyes, busted lips, and two miscarriages by him always putting his hands on me! So yeah, he gave me everything, but he can have it all back. I don't want it anymore. So yeah, he got what he deserved, and just because you raised him to be the man that he is, you're going to get what you deserve too."

Bishop walked up beside me and said, "This ain't the time for family therapy. Now let's get down to business. You came for Turtle, and I want those ki's. So let's get down to business."

I ignored Bishop. My anger was still on Turtle. I pulled a .380 from under my shirt. Everyone aimed their guns at me in alarm. I aimed the gun directly at Turtle, placing the barrel at his head. "Bishop, I'm going to kill Turtle, then I'm going to kill your homie beside you, then I'm going to go around the room killing each and every one until it's just me and you standing, then I'm going to kill you and show-case yo' death all over Instagram. How does that sound?" I asked without a care in the world.

Bishop laughed and said, "Ma, who do you think you are? Colombiana?" He laughed, causing all his goons to laugh as well.

I used my other hand to make my fingers into an image of a gun. The room got quiet, then they laughed as I pointed my fingers at Bishop's goon right beside him.

"What are you going to do with that?" Bishop asked. His goon walked up to me and placed his forehead to the tip of my finger, taunting me.

I smiled. *Bang!* I pulled the trigger, splattering Turtle's blood all over the back wall and floor. In an instant, Bishop's goon head snapped to the side, his body fell so fast everyone looked at my hand in shock. I aimed my gun at another goon and pulled the trigger, my finger aimed at another gun, and his body instantly fell, then the lights went black.

23

EMMANUEL

We all sat on the couch as we wondered what the next move would be. I sat on the couch between Hannah and Janice. I kinda felt like I had to separate them, or else Janice would've found an opportunity to slap the hell out of Hannah. Looking at Janice, she seemed to have forgotten that we were being held against our will, and at gunpoint, because all of her anger had been diverted to Hannah.

"Why are you here?" Janice said, finally being the one to break the awkward silence.

"We're here—" Squirrel began to say as Janice raised her left hand, silencing him, but at the same time, it caused Squirrel to laugh as her gesture caught him off guard.

"I was talking to her," Janice said, looking at Hannah with complete disgust.

"I should be asking you the same fuckin' question, seeing that this is my house!" Hannah shot back.

Janice shot to her feet and shouted, "Your house! You gave up your right to ownership when you let another man fuck you in the same bed you shared with your husband! Oh, my bad—Ex-husband!"

Hannah, not one to be outdone, jumped to her feet and pointed her finger in Janice's face. "Tramp, you couldn't wait to get your claws into my husband! I always knew—" Hannah was saying as Squirrel jumped in the middle of them.

"Would you two bitches, please . . . sit the fuck down! This ain't the Jerry Springer show, and I damn sho'll ain't no marriage counselor!" Squirrel said as he looked from Hannah to Janice, staring them both in the eyes, letting them know he meant business.

Janice grilled Hannah as she retook her seat beside me. Squirrel seemed to be upset about the whole encounter. Me, on the other hand, I was definitely enjoying the show. It was good for Hannah to see that another good, beautiful smart woman was interested in me. As I was thinking about the courage Janice had to express her hate to Hannah in such a drastic situation, something in me snapped. It wasn't courage, like Janice had shown, it wasn't strength, or the will to want to live. I honestly think it was the will to want to die with all the questions answered. As much as I really wanted to ask Hannah what the fuck she was doing here, I still had some questions I needed to answer.

"Squirrel, I mean, if I may call you by that name," I said, then cleared my throat. "Uhm, I know why you're here, but I thought that you came here alone. Now, I'm not from the streets, but I've represented a lot of people who actually are from the streets. If it was one thing that I learned by representing street guys, it is that when someone comes to kill someone, he goes at it alone. No face, no case, no witnesses, no testimony, right?"

Squirrel's reaction let me know that I had struck a chord. My words were music to his ears. Squirrel faced his comrade suspiciously and said, "What the fuck are you doing here, Bull? Who sent you?" Squirrel asked.

"Ken, he sent me to look after you," Bull said. Now, with all of my years as an attorney, I was good at reading people. I could instantly tell when people were lying, and I was damn sure good at seeing when people were nervous. And Bull was definitely nervous.

"Why would Ken send you to watch my back, when he never even was told I was coming here? No one knew I was coming here!" Squirrel said.

Bull, to me, looked nervous, but maybe Squirrel wasn't as good as I was at reading people. Bull hesitated momentarily, then he said, "Squirrel homie, don't start getting paranoid. Let's take care of business, and get the fuck out of here!" Bull said as he cocked his gun and aimed it at me.

By the look in Bull's eyes I knew then that I had ruined some kind of evil plan. And that alone let me know that I wasn't going to make it past the night. And with my big mouth, I would be the first to go. So if I had to die, I was going to die a free man. I wouldn't take Angel's deceitful lies with me to the grave. They weren't my secrets to keep; hell, I wanted no parts of them to begin with.

"Squirrel, earlier before we were interrupted with my lousy attempt to escape, you had asked me a very important question. You had asked if one of the feds had made, or asked me to send Ken off to prison."

"And, you said no," Squirrel said.

"Exactly!" I said, happy that he was in fact entertaining my conversation. "It wasn't the feds, Squirrel," I said, hoping and praying that he could read between the lines.

"So, if it wasn't the feds, then who the hell was it?" Squirrel asked as he sat on the edge of his seat.

"Someone did in fact tell—no, made me throw Ken's case, but it wasn't the feds."

"Man, fuck what this nigga talkin' 'bout. Squirrel, let's kill these ma'fuckas and be out!" Bull said, agitated.

"I want to hear this! Because if a nigga betrayed Ken, then they betrayed me too!" Squirrel said, raising his voice.

I looked at Squirrel with a lot of hate, but with a little respect. He was loyal to Ken. So, I told him the truth. "Deceit hurts, but it hurts ten times more when it comes from your own wife," I said as I dazed off, thinking about how Hannah had deceived me. I was a first-hand witness to betrayal.

"Wife!" Squirrel spat. "So, you're saying, Ang—"

Baka! Baka!

Two shots rang out, both pushing their way through Squirrel's back. Squirrel's gold teeth were dripping red with his own blood. Squirrel's eyes looked as if they were about to pop out of their sockets. Now Squirrel was a witness to deceit. He was now a living witness to betrayal.

Squirrel's body fell forward, Bull stood behind him with his gun now aimed at me. Janice had to have been in shock, because she didn't utter a word. Hannah on the other hand screamed as if she was auditioning for the opera.

"Shut . . .! The . . . fuck . . . up!" Bull screamed at Hannah. "Now, if y'all don't want to end up like Squirrel, you'll shut the fuck up, and do exactly as I say!" Bull said.

I looked at Bull as he looked around the room. I could see the look in his eyes. He was indeed a killer. This wasn't his first body, I could tell. The reason I knew was because he wasn't panicking. He wasn't nervous one bit. He knew he had the entire situation under control. He knew it because he was the only person in the room with a gun. And we were first-hand witnesses; he wasn't afraid to use it.

I looked down at Squirrel's gun. My eyes locked onto it. I felt that I had no other choice. I was Janice's only hope, and sadly to say, Hannah's too. I looked at Bull trying to determine the distance between me, him, and Squirrel's gun. Bull looked up at me as if he was reading my thoughts. His eyes traveled to Squirrel's gun.

"Don't even think about it. I'm telling you, I didn't come to play no fuckin' games, feel me. Like they used to say in school, '*reach one, teach one!*'" Bull said. I nodded as I relaxed on the couch. If I was our only hope, then we had just become hopeless. I wanted to help us, but not at the extent of me dying. If I was to die trying to help Janice and Hannah, I would be one angry dead bastard to find out that they didn't make it out alive.

"Okay, get up!" Bull demanded. Janice snapped out of her trance as Hannah looked at me as if she was waiting on me to do something stupid. "Lawyer boy, move the table so we can wrap this bitch ass nigga up with the rug. I would kill y'all here with this nigga and burn the whole fuckin' house down, but we don't want anything to come back to Angel, do we." He laughed. "So, let's go, all of y'all!" he said as he waved his gun from left to right. Each time Bull would wave his gun in Hannah's direction, she would duck and place her hands high above her head.

Janice would look at Hannah sideways each time she would do it. It made me laugh on the inside each time. But, as I tried to keep my composure, I stood up and looked down at Janice and Hannah for them to do the same. There was only one thing left to do, and that was to listen to every command Bull gave us. In a way, I felt that I was being bullied by Angel all over again. I wasn't the one that shot Squirrel, even though God knows I wanted to, badly. But, here I was, again . . . being bullied at gunpoint, again . . . helping someone get rid of the evidence. I swear this was the worst case of déjà vu!

24

ANGEL

As the lights went out, the gunfire inside the garage stopped. Everyone was afraid to shoot the wrong person, so all gunfire ceased. Then a loud deafening shot sounded off, causing all of Bishop's goons to focus their aim in that direction. As Bishop's goons fired, the sparks from the barrels of their guns lit up the dark night as the sounds of bullet shells erupted like a new NBA YoungBoy song.

I hid behind the Monte Carlo as I watched Bishop from a distance. Bishop's face reflected off the night sky as he looked around for me. As he looked for me, the rest of his goons did their damndest to fight off Luis' goons. As I crouched behind the Monte Carlo, I took out the last dummy bullet from my gun and replaced it with all hollow point bullets. I cocked the gun back quietly and slowly so that I wouldn't give up my position.

I really wanted to kill Turtle's old ass, but with Luis' goons watching, I couldn't. So, I came up with a plan; a diversion, if I could say. I shot Turtle in the head with a rubber bullet. Now don't get me wrong, the blood was real, and so was the pain, because I shot him close range, but he would live, hopefully.

As I crept around the car towards Turtle, my foot knocked over a glass bottle. I cursed myself under my breath as I tried to be still.

Bishop heard the bottle and followed his ears towards me. I wasn't sure if he could see me or not, but I wasn't going to take any chances.

I cased under the Monte Carlo and watched as Bishop stood where I had been momentarily before. I aimed my gun at his legs. I only had one good shot; missing would be to declare my own death. I don't know why, but the lights came back on. It seemed as if all the gunfire in the room had stopped. As I lay perfectly still under the Monte Carlo. I only counted two sets of legs, one being Bishop's. I could see Bishop looking around at all the dead bodies.

"She's alive, I can feel it!" Bishop said as he stepped over a dead body.

Bishop moved closer to Turtle; he leaned down and saw that Turtle was still breathing. Bishop rubbed his thumb across Turtle's forehead. The blood on Turtle's forehead smeared, but it was then that Bishop noticed there wasn't a hole in Turtle's forehead, only a gash.

"That bitch!" Bishop said as he cocked his gun and placed it at the center of Turtle's forehead.

As bad as I wanted to see Turtle's old ass dead, I couldn't let Bishop be the one to do it. I needed Turtle alive, that's if I wanted my plan to work.

I fired off a single shot. The bullet caught Bishop in his ankle. His screams were deafening. The element of surprise caught Bishop by surprise. Bishop let off a simple shot, but his momentum made the gun rise, and the bullet went through the front windshield of the Monte Carlo.

As soon as the bullet smashed through Bishop's ankle, I seized the opportunity and crawled from under the Monte Carlo. I crawled so fast you would've sworn I was in the military.

"You bitch, ahh, you dirty sneaky bitch!" Bishop screamed as he used his strength to balance himself on the Monte Carlo.

I loved guns and the power they held. When men looked at me they saw a bad, thick boss bitch. But when they saw me, the bad, thick boss bitch with a gun, they gave me a new look. A look of respect.

"I love that word. Bitch!" I said as I walked up to Bishop. My gun was held tight in my hand as I walked up to him. I was without fear. I wasn't hiding anymore as I walked up to him boldly with my gun in hand.

Bishop did little to prevent the inevitable. The little energy he had he used it to hold himself up. Bishop's last goon wasn't a goon, but his computer cousin—Wiz. He wasn't a threat to no one but a computer virus. Wiz stood on the side with his iPhone and laptop in hand, scared, skating like a stripper.

"You know you'sa sneaky lil bitch, huh!" Bishop said with a smile of defeat on his face. Bishop was one of those niggas that smiled when he knew he had lost. His smile, to him, made the pain seem less painful. But I could see past his mask, I could see the pain clearly on his face.

"See, see!" Bishop said through pants. "See, that's why I wanted to meet you. Tha-that's exactly why I wanted you to make the delivery. I had heard rumors, stories about the solid woman Ken had molded. I thought the rumors were only a myth!" Bishop said, then laughed.

"But, you're exactly what people said you were."

Bishop continued.

"You know, you can't believe everything you hear, huh?" I said as I leaned on the side of the Monte Carlo. I leaned on the side of him, taunting him. I looked at Wiz; he stood in the open, his phone in hand, scared of what was to come. "Bishop, since you had the balls to take on Ken, I will grant you two choices. Either I kill you, or your cousin could kill you. But, Wiz, if you kill him, you get to live. Deal?" I said without looking in Bishop's direction.

"Look at you being noble. How about I just kill you?" Bishop said as his breathing got worse.

"Cut the b-s, Bishop. You and I both know I caught you lacking. Your body is getting weaker by the second. You're barely able to hold yourself up. So, if I'm guessing right, I hit an artery. So your stunting is on borrowed time. So, your choice, yo' people, or me. What's it going to be?" Bishop sighed. He knew I was right. I had caught him lacking, and now he was paying for it, with his life. Bishop gained as much strength as he could and took a deep breath. "Wiz!" Bishop called out to his cousin.

Wiz shook his head. Tears had begun to fall down his face. I watched from a close distance as the two reminded me of a *Lifetime* movie network scene.

"Wiz, you have to. You have to!" Bishop struggled to say.

Wiz continued to shake his head with tears streaming down his face. Bishop seemed to have sling strength, and I became irritated by the whole situation. "Wi-z," Bishop panted. As Bishop said his last words, his arm slipped off the car as his body fell to the ground.

"Tsk-tsk-tsk," I said as I shook my head at Wiz. "Wiz, Wiz, Wiz," I added as I walked over Bishop's body in Wiz's direction. Wiz slowly took cautious steps backwards. He wiped his face as he looked down at his lifeless cousin, then his attention was averted to me, the attractive woman that was holding the murder weapon that had killed his cousin.

"Wiz, you can't say I didn't give you an honest chance," I said as I raised the gun to the range of Wiz's face. "We could've really been a good team. A bitch like me could've really used a computer wiz like you. But I don't care what position you play in my circle. You have to have heart. And heart you don't have!"

Baka! Baka!

I shot Wiz once in the head. The second bullet caught him in the chin as his body fell. I looked around the garage; I was the lone one standing. As I walked towards Turtle, I heard a faint gasp by the garage door. I held my gun steady as I crept towards the faint noise. Another notch on my belt of bodies was my goal.

I neared the entrance, I noticed Filipe on the ground; his shirt was stained with blood, his bullet-proof vest wasn't able to catch every bullet that was thrown at him. I kneeled over Filipe as I laid my gun down beside him.

"Filipe, can you stand?" I asked, as I looked for where the bullet had entered. The bullet had struck him in his left shoulder, right above the Velcro vest straps.

"Yes, I can stand," Filipe said as he held his left shoulder, putting pressure on the bullet wound. I used all of my strength to help him stand. Filipe stood and looked around at the dirty job he had been enlisted to do. "Wow," was all Filipe could say as he used my shoulder for a crutch. And *wow* was right, we had come to do a job, and a job well done we did.

"Where's Turtle, is he okay?" Filipe asked as I opened the passenger side door to the Monte Carlo. I helped him sit down. Filipe grunted like he had been shot in the heart.

"He's over there on the ground acting like I really shot him, hell." I laughed as I walked around the car to check on Turtle's old ass. I nudged him with my feet to try to wake him up. I didn't understand what had him sleep in the first place. Then again I figured he was playing dead.

"Turtle!" I yelled. He continued to act like he couldn't hear me. I looked around on the ground for something to dash Turtle's faking ass with. I found a half-empty beer bottle. I picked the bottle up and held it over Turtle's face, turning it upside down I poured the last of the beer all over Turtle's face.

Turtle kicked and rose up like he had just been resuscitated after almost drowning. Turtle balanced himself up with the palm of his hands as he looked around the room at all the casualties. People that had sacrificed their lives to save him, and he didn't know their names. Then Turtle's hand shot to his forehead. He gaped at the pain, and he felt around for a hole, but there was only a gash. Then he looked at me and said, "You shot me!" Filipe managed to laugh. "I saved yo' life. So what if I shot you! At least I didn't kill you. So?" I said as I held my hand out to help him to his feet. Turtle stood and took another look around as he tried to gather himself. As he dusted himself off, he looked at Filipe and said, "Filipe, I'm sorry for the men you lost, and I'm very grateful for your loyalty and sacrifice."

I placed my hands on my hips. This nigga had some nerve. He thanked Filipe like he was the mastermind behind his rescue. I cleared my throat, loud and disgustingly. I wanted to make sure he heard me, and I wanted to make sure I had his undivided attention.

Turtle faced me, with his ugly short ass. "It's nice of you to be giving out shout outs and what not, but when you start giving out thanks, make sure my name is mentioned first!"

"Angel, patience is a virtue. You know that, right?" Turtle said as he walked up to me and wrapped his arms around me, hugging me tightly.

I almost felt bad for what I had planned for him. Turtle never showed me any affection. Hell, he never showed anyone any affection. The last hug he gave out was to me and Ken, and that was at our wedding. But, being a good sneaky wife, I hugged him back.

"Thank you, Angel."

As I relaxed under his embrace, my phone began to ring. I sighed as I looked at the screen, it was Bull. I hated how I had given him the time of day. Even though he was only a pawn in the game, he was a sacrificial pawn. One that would never make it to the other side to be anything greater. I wasn't putting him to a place he didn't deserve to be; he belonged there. Hell, if he had taken care of Turtle like I had instructed him to, I would've never been in this predicament. But being that he was a part of the game, I still had to answer the phone. Lord knows I didn't want to.

25

BULL

I stood over Squirrel as he laid rolled up in lawyer boy rug. I wasn't covered in blood because I used most of my energy waving the gun around, giving out orders and shouting demands. Lawyer boy and his snow bunny seemed to take orders well. But the pretty petite Asian bitch wouldn't stop crying. Every time she would lift his body up, she would drop him just as fast.

As bad as I didn't want to, we laid Squirrel in the trunk of my car. I thought about using Squirrel's car, but I would have to leave my own car, and leaving my car at a murder scene wasn't going to happen.

"Get in," I said to lawyer boy and his—I don't know. I guess you could call them his hoes. By the look of lawyer boy, I wouldn't have taken him for a pimp. But I could see by the way they looked at them, they both loved him. But when lawyer boy looked at them, I got a different vibe when he looked at them. When he looked at the petite

Asian, he looked as if he cared, but he could live without her. Like if he could only save one of them, he would jump in to save the white one. I knew that by the way he looked at her. He looked at her the same way I looked at Angel, like he would do anything for her. Even if it meant killing someone like I did.

"Come on, man, just let us go. We won't say anything, I mean we can't, we're accessory to murder already as it is. We'll be telling on ourselves if we tell on you." Lawyer boy tried to reason.

"You go when I say you can go!" I said as I pointed my gun at him. "Now get in the fuckin' car!" I yelled. My patience was past running thin; it had run, and nothing could catch it.

Lawyer boy and his two hunnies all tried to get in the back seat. I looked at Asian persuasion and said, "Ying yang, get yo' pretty self in the front."

She looked at lawyer boy for his approval. He nodded, not like he had much say-so in the decision. I waited until everyone was seated before I took my seat behind the wheel. As I closed the door, I noticed how quiet the car was. And people say chaos only equals chaos.

I cranked the car to life and pulled away from lawyer boy's house. I grabbed my phone from the middle console and dialed Angel's number. I smiled as I looked at the screen. I only hoped she would be proud.

———

Emmanuel

I SAT behind Bull as Janice sat beside me, and Hannah sat quietly in the passenger seat. Bull pulled away from my house. I looked back at my house thinking that it would be the last time I was to see it. As Bull drove away, he pulled out his phone and dialed a number. I looked at all the houses as we passed them by. I couldn't believe my life had come to this.

Bull began to speak into his phone. Whoever he was talking to, he told them that he had me, along with two others. He also stated that Squirrel had been present when he showed up to take care of me. He actually said *take care of me*. I wasn't sick, so I knew what he meant by *take care*. Bull had been sent to kill me. I knew that Squirrel was there on behalf of Kendrick. I knew that because Squirrel was very specific on why I had done what I did getting Kendrick so much time. So if Squirrel was there for Kendrick, then Bull was there for Angel.

I took a deep breath as I listened to Bull as he asked what he was supposed to do next. If it really was Angel on the other end, I can guarantee she told Bull to finish the job. Angel knew I was her only loose end, a loose end she wanted tightened up.

Bull agreed to whatever was orchestrated and hung up the phone. He looked at me through the rearview mirror. I looked down, pretending I didn't know what was going on. I wish I was in the passenger seat beside him. I knew he had his gun in his lap within reach.

Bull turned the radio up; he began to nod to the beat. He was enjoying himself. How could someone who had a dead body in the trunk and three other hostages be so happy like he did nothing wrong.

I looked at Janice; she looked past Hannah looking out the front windshield. Janice was in a daze, most likely thinking the same shit I was recently thinking. How did her life come to this? A beautiful, young lawyer's assistant who worked her entire life to become a defense lawyer. Her only bad decision was working for me as my assistant. It's crazy how one life decision can help, or hurt you for the rest of your life.

Then there was my cheating ass wife, Hannah. A woman who had a get-out-of-jail free card, and decided she wanted back in. Maybe this was her punishment for cheating on me. A need she will never get fulfilled. A want she will never have. She had loved and lost, now I bet she wished she had never loved at all. Then, there was the unborn baby growing inside of Hannah's stomach. The only one out of all of us that's really innocent. The only one incapable of making its own decisions. The more I thought of the baby, the more I made myself hate Hannah. I cared for the baby, because there was a chance it could be mine. Then again, there was a chance it could be my ex-best friend's. God, how tacky it would be if the baby wasn't mine. If it was mine, I would take care of it. I know Janice would still love me no matter what. Thinking about the baby made me think about what kind of father I wanted to be. It was always hard imagining the father you wanted to be, especially when you never experienced being a father before. Yet, it was easy knowing the type of father you didn't want to be. Like I knew I didn't want to be an absent father. And I'm not saying that because I'm in a dire situation. I'm saying it because it's true. I never had my father. Even though I came out pretty decent, I still needed him.

That's why if the baby Hannah was carrying was mine, I was going to be there.

Something inside of me began to rise. Something deep within my soul began to stir. It wasn't the want, or the need to live. It was the want and need to be a father. Something I always wanted. Something I really, really needed at the moment. Something to live for. I looked to the front seat to Hannah. As if she could read my mind, she placed her left hand over her belly, as if she was protecting our unborn seed. I looked to Janice; she stared out the window trying to be tough, but even strength was no match for her tears.

I looked to the driver's seat at Bull. He was in a full rap zone as he drove through the streets. It was guys like him that made me regret being a defense attorney. I should've been a district attorney locking people like him up, not keeping them out. But now I had the chance to put him away forever. And I wasn't about to pass this opportunity up.

I sat up straight, careful so that Bull wouldn't notice. My sudden movement caught Janice's attention. She wiped her eyes as she looked at me. I grabbed her hand, squeezing it tight. Without words I just wanted her to know how much I loved her. I waited for the perfect time. I only had one opportunity; one fuck up, and we were all dead. Deep down I knew if I didn't do anything, we would all be dead anyway. So I made my move.

"Arghh!" I screamed as I grabbed Bull's seatbelt and wrapped it around his neck tightly as I pulled. I don't know why I screamed, but it did feel like it gave me a little courage.

The element of surprise caught everyone in the car by surprise. Bull swerved through the four-way intersection as he tried to keep the car straight; at the same time he clawed at my hands to try to loosen my grip. As if Bull remembered he had his gun on his lap, he reached for it. Hannah reacted, grabbing the gun first. There was so much going on, and everything happened so fast neither of us had any time to react as we crashed head-on to a Dodge pickup in the middle of the intersection. Before my head smashed into the front headrest, I heard a loud popping sound. Without mistaking, I knew it to be a gunshot.

———

Angel

AS MY PHONE began to ring. I looked at the screen; it was Bull calling. I had sent him on a mission, one that was supposed to be easily handled, so I wasn't understanding why he was calling. I had already given him instructions. I liked Bull. He was trainable, handsome, but he lacked the energy. I'm not sure how to say it; he lacked the thug I was so used to. The aggressiveness I was used to. I didn't like for a man to hit me, but I didn't mind being roughed up when I stepped out of line. You know, snatch me up by my ponytail, grab my arm, even muff me. Show me you're in control. Hell, Bull—he was a killer, I'll give him that, but he was super soft when it came to women, or should I just say me.

"Turtle, Imma take this call, never know it could be

Kendrick," I said as I hid the phone screen from his view. Turtle nodded as he went over to help Filipe.

Once he got out of earshot, I said, "Tell me something good."

"I got the package, but he came with two others. I didn't really have a choice." Bull spoke into the phone.

"Take care of it all, I'm serious," I whispered

"I got a problem though. When I came to take care of the problem, I ran into another one. Squirrel was there when I pulled up. He was interrogating the lawyer, on behalf of Ken!" Bull said.

His words brought so many stress lines to my face, I was sure I'd aged in just seconds. "Okay, take care of it all. I'll tap in once I leave here. Be safe!" I said, looking over my shoulder to make sure Turtle or Filipe didn't hear.

"Take care of your business, and don't worry, I'ma take care of everything here."

I hung up and sighed. If it wasn't one thing, it was another. I cleaned my mood up and walked over to Filipe and Turtle. "Y'all ready?" I asked. "We should leave, and fast. I think we've overstayed our welcome."

Turtle nodded as he and Filipe leaned on each other for support. I opened the driver's door to the Monte Carlo and raised the seat forward. Filipe eased into the back as Turtle walked around the front to the passenger seat. As Turtle sat down, I looked around at the garage of dead bodies. The news was going to have a field day with this, I was sure.

As I closed the door and cranked the engine to life, Turtle looked at me and asked, "Angel, are there really over a hundred ki's in that U-Haul across the street?"

I backed out the warehouse, peeping over my shoulders

to make sure one of Bishop's goons didn't outlive my bullets. "Nah, I didn't come with nothing but five ki's. That's the five that's under the hood of the car, tucked deeply behind the engine."

"If I'm not mistaken, they had requested that you bring two hundred ki's in exchange for me. Didn't they?" Turtle asked.

I nodded. "Yeah, that's exactly what they asked for."

"So why didn't you bring them? What if they would've killed me because you didn't follow their orders?" Turtle said, obviously upset.

I found myself laughing at him. I didn't have to turn my head in order to see him eyeing me. I could feel his eyes mugging me. Since he didn't find my laughter appropriate, he said, "What was funny about what I said?"

"The fact that you think you're worth two hundred ki's. That's what's funny. Do you hear yo'self. Hell, I was amazed to even hear they asked for that much in exchange for you. Like, who the fuck they thought you were. To even think you should be handed over for that much dope is outrageous and selfish." I knew I was a little harsh, but I mean he had to hear the truth for once in his life. I knew he was always used to hearing what he wanted to hear. I wasn't that kind of bitch. I was the bitch that spoke her mind, no matter who I was talking to.

"It's women like you that should only be born with two holes, cause your third one will have a man under a prison for the rest of his natural born life."

I laughed at him again. He had no idea how true his words were. "Bitch, laugh one more 'gain!" Turtle said.

His words finally drew a reaction out of me. I looked

over at him as I was driving through a green light. As I was about to say something, a bright light shined from behind me. The light moved at us faster than the wind. Next thing I knew, my entire body whipped to the right, then hard to the left as we were hit by something. My head hit the airbag, and my vision became dark.

The pain was excruciating. It felt as if I had dislocated my hip. The passenger door opened. I couldn't see anything. I could barely move. My hearing wasn't impaired as I heard a man's voice say:

"Get 'em out, fast. Let's go!" the first man said.

"What about the one in the back?" another man asked.

"Kill him!" the first man said. I tried to move my legs; only the right one would move. It seemed like my entire left side was numb. Blood covered and clogged my eyes, blocking my vision.

Baka! Baka!

Two loud gunshots rang out behind me. By the gunshots being so close, I knew they had shot Filipe in the head.

"What about the girl?" the gunman asked. I was in so much pain, I couldn't plead for my life no matter how hard I wanted to.

A noise came from beside me. It sounded like they were dragging Turtle from the car, "Boss, the girl?" the gunman asked again.

"N-oo," Turtle said as they dragged him out of the car. I wasn't sure if he had said no for them to leave him alone, or to leave me alone. Either way, I wasn't killed. But as they dragged me from the car, the pain from my body made me wish I was dead. My body felt helpless as I was tossed in the back of a truck. As the truck pulled off, I could feel my body giving into the pain. I felt tired, super tired. It was easy for me to go into the darkness, my eyes were already closed.

26

EMMANUEL

"Arghh!" I grunted in pain as I held on to my arm. My head was throbbing, my vision was blurry, and I knew without a doubt my arm was broken. It seemed like everything had happened so fast. All I could remember was me looking at Janice's face just before I used Bull's seatbelt as a weapon to strangle him with.

As I was strangling Bull, I could feel his nails clawing at my hands. I could feel his nails breaking through flesh, drawing blood, but I was motivated, numb to the pain. Then Bull reached for his gun, and so did Hannah. Neither of us was paying attention to what side of the street we were on, or the truck that was coming head-on with us, until we crashed. My eyes managed to open. I looked to the side of me to Janice. Janice's head was leaning on the cracked passenger door window. Her chest rose up and down slowly, so I knew she was alive. I tried to stay as quiet as possible, I didn't want to alarm Bull, if he was still alive. Leaning forward, I looked to the front seats. I closed my eyes as I took in a deep breath. The entire front dash had been pushed in, maybe three inches. Glass was all over Bull and Hannah. I could see Bull's hand; the gun was still in it.

Using my right hand, I opened my side door. My legs were functioning fine as I eased out the car. I walked to the front of the car holding my limp left arm. The driver of the Dodge pickup looked to still be alive as he couldn't stop coughing from the cloud of smoke coming from the hood of his truck. I looked through the shattered windshield of Bull's car. There was no movement coming from him or Hannah. The driver of the Dodge shoved his door open as he stumbled out and fell to the ground.

I remained still in front of the wreck. I really wanted to break down and wait until the police came and tell them everything from beginning to end. Then I realized that if Bull had in fact died from the wreck, then I was going up shits creek without a paddle. With Bull being alive, it would be easy to point fingers but if he was dead, then all fingers would be pointed at me.

My head turned to the sound of the close but distant fire truck sounds. With them being close, I knew the police couldn't be too far behind. I ran around the back of Bull's car to Janice's door. I opened the door, not thinking about Bull. If he was alive, and if he was to see me making my escape, would he shoot me in the back like a rogue, racist cop?

I moved Janice's head to the side, brushing small shards of glass from her cheek and face. "Janice, wake up, we have to go." I squeezed her left leg, then the right to see if she would jump from the pain, yet she didn't.

Janice's eyes opened and closed, then opened again as she looked up at me. She looked as if she was imagining me. As if I wasn't standing in front of her. "Janice, we have to hurry. Can you walk?" I asked as I helped her lean forward.

Janice's hand went to her head. She winced in pain.

"Emmanuel, what happened?"

"We crashed, okay. The police are coming. We have to get Hannah, and go quickly. Can you stand?" I asked as I looked to the front seat to make sure Bull was still passed out.

"I-I think so," Janice said as she began to gather herself. I used my good arm to help her stand. As Janice stood, I began to see the lights from the fire truck getting closer.

"Wait here, I'll get Hannah," I said as I gave Janice the once-over. She looked to have received some pretty bad injuries to her head. Her arm was bleeding, but she was okay for the matter.

I ducked my head to the passenger seat to get Hannah. I opened the door, which took a lot of strength. I looked to Bull. I couldn't make out if he was dead or alive. Deep down I was praying he was dead, then again I hoped he was alive, so he could suffer for the rest of his life in prison.

"Hannah, Hannah, can you hear me? We have to go," I whispered as I leaned over her to unbuckle her seat belt. I looked down at the seat belt and noticed there was blood all over the middle of the seat belt.

Hannah began to stir as she looked up at me. Slow tears began to fall down her cheeks. I knew everything that had happened had her worked up. If I didn't have to be strong for the both of them, I would probably cry too.

"I know you're upset, Hannah, but we have to go. The police are coming, there's a dead body in the trunk. If they come and we're still here, we're all going to jail!" I said as I tried to help her up.

It seemed as if my words made her cry even more. I couldn't just sit by and watch her cry until the police came, so I pulled her out of the car with my good arm. As she stood, I noticed her midsection was covered with blood. Then it all really hit me. The scuffle between her and Bull for the gun, just before it went off. The blood covered just a spot that surrounded a small hole in her shirt. Hannah looked at me with pleading eyes. I knew the reason she looked at me the way she did. I had the same thoughts, but now wasn't the time to think, so I pushed the thoughts to the back of my mind.

"Manny, the—the baby. What if something happened to the baby?" Hannah cried hysterically.

I placed my finger to my lips hoping she would be quiet. "Shhh, Hannah, we have to go," I said as I looked over to make sure Janice was okay. In that brief moment from me looking away, I faced Hannah again to calm her down. I looked behind her to Bull. It was as if my worst nightmare had become my reality. Time had slowed down. I could hear the sirens in the distance, oil from Bull's engine dripping. I could even feel the air coursing through my body. The same air that had me alive, as well as Bull.

I finally realized what *DayDay* meant when he said the air tastes different, because this air had a taste of its own. The taste was bitter, and sweet. I had made it through the crash, and so did Bull. And as it seemed as if I had slowed time down, I wasn't moving fast enough to stop what was to come.

So I began to yell. The words came out much slower than they ever had. To only be two letters, they sure carried a lot of weight. As bad as the pain was in my arm I still used it to try to move Hannah out the way. Hannah looked into my eyes as the bullet slammed into her spine. The impact caused her to fall onto me. I caught her as her knees began to give out.

I looked over my shoulder to Bull; it seemed as he had used all of his strength to shoot Hannah as his head leaned back against the seat, and the gun fell at his side. Hannah's body became heavy as we sank to the ground. Blood slowly began to creep out the corners of her mouth.

"I - I'm sorry," Hannah said as blood specks splashed from her mouth to my face.

Although Hannah had brought me great pain by cheating with my best friend, that was temporary pain. Something I knew I would one day get over. But seeing the pain in her eyes, the way her tears seemed to be slowly giving away right along with her breathing, I didn't know I was crying until one of my tears fell on her cheek.

"Shh, Hannah. Everything is going to be okay. None of this is your fault. I'm the one to blame. I'm the one to blame!" I said as I looked up to the sky. If I had an extra leg, I would kick myself. Even though my words were meant to soothe her, they were true. All of this was my fault. No matter who I tried to blame, it was my fault. I should've reported Angel the very first night. I was a lawyer; people would've believed me. And if there was a worst case scenario, if they didn't believe me, I would convince them; that was my job. Now it was too late.

I shook my head side to side, afraid to look down, knowing the woman I loved dearly was gone. But not wanting to live with the truth, I kept my head held high as I cradled her in my arms. Even with my eyes closed I could still see the police lights as they got closer.

"Emmanuel, if we're going to go, then we have to go."

"But I can't leave her, not like this. She's still my wife."

I know I shouldn't have yelled, but it was either yell, or breakdown. I would never be able to build myself back up. Janice just looked at me, then she looked to the dancing lights that bounced off the top of the police and ambulances. She then took a seat beside me. As Hannah's head rested on my leg, my head rested on Janice's shoulder. I didn't know what was to come of us now. Once the police had us in custody, I knew our faces would be plastered all over every local news, maybe even world news. Even though I was new to being locked up, I still knew the procedure, and so did Janice. We had the right to remain silent, anything we said or did would be used against us in court. And that's where the Miranda rights would stop. Because there was no need for an attorney, I was already present.

27

ANGEL

"Ahhhhh!" I grunted as I came to. I opened my eyes, blinking them to get adjusted to the light, but there was none. My eyes were covered with some kind of scarf or blindfold. There was a small glimmer of light but not enough to see through it.

"Look who woke up," a voice said from inside the room. I wiggled in my restraints, hoping to loosen them. I had little luck as the rope seemed to have cut at my wrist.

Another man said, "Queen bee, you finally come back to reality, huh?" I couldn't make out either of their voices. All I could do was stay quiet and hope to God they would give themselves up.

"Should we go get the boss?" the first man asked.

"Yeah, he's been waiting for her to wake up," the second man said. The sound of the man's shoes could be heard on the hardwood floor as he left the room to retrieve his boss.

"When he gets here, please don't lie to him. If you do,

I'll be the one to beat the truth out of you!" the man said as he kneeled down in front of me. "And just so you know, I take pride in beating the truth out of people."

"Hey, get out her face like that!" another man said as he entered the room. The voice sounded all too familiar. This voice sounded like Turtle's voice.

"I'm sorry, boss. I was just warming her up for you, that's all."

"Take that off of her face," the bossman demanded.

As soon as the blindfold was lifted from my eyes, I hung my head to protect my eyes from the light. I had to have been knocked out for a day or two, considering how sensitive my eyes were to the light. Once my vision adjusted, I lifted my eyes to the true definition of betrayal.

"Turtle!" I said as I tried to stand up. My legs were tied, as well as my arms. Turtle stood before me with a gray Tom Ford suit on along with some gray Gators. He held his stance with a gold and gray cane. Last I recalled, he didn't have a need for a cane, so I'm guessing it was the car crash that caused the damage.

"Turtle, you snake. I can't believe you! After all we did to come and save you, you pull this bullshit on me. Wait 'til Ken hears about this!" I was angry, but not as angry as I was embarrassed.

Turtle held this dumb smirk on his face as he held himself up with his cane. I had every intention of slapping the smirk right off his face the first chance I got. "What's wrong? Angel don't like to be double crossed?" Turtle said, then laughed.

"*Double crossed*. You're an old fool! In order for me to

have been double crossed, it would mean I'd had crossed you, and I never have."

Turtle balanced the cane with two hands, placing the right above the left. "Angel, the day I was kidnapped, I saw Kendrick's young muscle tailing me from the golf course. As much as he tried to blend in, he failed terribly. It was just by chance those bums snatched me up first. See, my security noticed the young muscle tailing us. We were just waiting for him to make his move, then he was going to be in the same seat that you're in right now. I'm guessing you're not going to tell.

"Who says I know anything to tell?" I played along.

Turtle laughed. "Kendrick always said you were the reflection of him."

"And he was right!" I said with pride.

"I know Kendrick's already in a prison cell, laughing, thinking I'm already dead. After all I did for him. I raised him as my own son, gave him everything, taught him everything. I even left him the game to play with his own rules. And he goes and stabs me in the back for what, two hundred kilos!" Turtle shouted.

There was nothing for me to say. I stayed silent as Turtle vented about some shit he really had no clue of. Here he was shouting how Kendrick had betrayed him, and Kendrick was more loyal to him than he was to his own wife. I placed that together when Kendrick let me make the exchange to get Turtle back. And then he has the nerve to say two hundred kilos! Hell yeah! People get killed these days for less. Betrayal has been on sale for a long time, with a seventy-five percent discount.

"So you have nothing to say? Huh!" Turtle shouted.

I grilled him from my front row seat. He wasn't scaring me. From where I was sitting, I had the upper hand. Me being alive only told me I had something he wanted. And whatever it was, I wasn't coming off of it without a fair fight.

"What is it that you want from me, Turtle? You already got this fabricated story in your mind about how me and Kendrick crossed you for two hundred ki's. Which to me is stupid."

"How is it stupid?" Turtle asked.

"Cause, bald head ass coon, why would we snake you for two hundred ki's and then still come to save you? How dumb does that sound? Make it make sense!"

"Make this make sense, Angel." Turtle said as he pulled out a manilla envelope. He opened it and pulled out some pictures. He tossed the pictures on the floor in front of me, one at a time.

The first picture was of Bull, Pistol, and Kendrick just laughing and kicking it. The next one was of Bull standing outside of Ken's trap house. Then he tossed a picture of me. I was being escorted back to my car by Bull. I can still remember the day like it was yesterday.

"I'm not understanding this. You're taking pictures of us like you're the feds, why?" I asked.

"Because, I like to know what's going on around me, even when you're not around me, that's why."

"Those pictures still don't explain anything," I said.

"That's why you're sitting here. And you're going to sit here until you explain everything to me!" Turtle said.

"There's nothing to explain," I said, defeated. I felt like I was going in circles with him, and I was the only one getting dizzy from it. He wanted me to give him the answers to the questions he never asked. The shit didn't make any sense to me.

"Explain to me where the two hundred kilos are," Turtle said. Now he was starting to make sense. See, I knew he had me alive for something. And now that I knew what it was, I could counter him, and call his bluff.

"What two hundred kilos?" I said, then smirked.

"Why, you little bitch!" Turtle yelled as he reared back with his cane and slammed it smack against the side of my head. My eyes rolled to the back of my head. In the darkness my mind couldn't help but remember how Turtle had said he taught Kendrick everything he knew. I'm sure that wasn't a lie, because they both had hitting women in common. As I sat in his chair, I only had one regret. I regret that I had placed rubber bullets in that clip.

28

TURTLE

"Boss, do you think she's dead?" my youngest soldier, Nico, asked. Nico was my late right hand man's oldest son. Nico was already in training by his father but once his father lost his life to protect me, I did what any loyal comrade would do. I pulled his son close and since then, I've been doing my best to show him the way his father would've. In so many ways Nico reminded me of his father. The only thing: Nico talked way too much.

"She's alive. I'm sure of it. Nobody in their right mind would die that easily knowing you have two hundred kilos stashed some place," I said as I watched her chest slowly find a steady pace. Once I noticed she was alive, I walked out the room with Nico on my tail.

"Boss, I didn't think you were going to come out and let her know you knew. I thought you were going to sit in the background and watch everything unfold!" Nico said with a grin on his face.

Like I said, Nico reminded me a lot of his father. Each

time Nico would say something he thought was clever, he too would also smile for his own personal reason. Nico took after his father with his looks too.

Nico adopted his father's build. Nico was heavy-set, but much more on the lineman muscle build. He had the weight, but you could tell the muscle was there just lurking for its time to come out to play. Nico was the same age as Kendrick. In fact, they attended the same school, and they were as tight as a closed fist growing up. They were raised together because Nico was always with me. Kendrick and Nico being close only was right. Something happened between Kendrick and Nico right after graduation that caused them to take separate paths; I'm not too privy on the details. Honestly, I never asked. But being that his father was always my right hand, Nico always had what he needed in the game; he just never used it.

But I stood and thought about Nico's question. In the beginning, I was going to just sit back and let everything unfold. All the lies, disloyalty, and backstabbing. But then I thought about how being stabbed in the back would hurt worse. To me, pain hurt less when you knew it was coming. So yeah, I came to the party, but I didn't come without party gifts. Kidnapping Angel was just the beginning.

"I thought about sitting in the back, being the director, watching my work unfold right before my eyes," I said as I joined in and grinned.

"So why didn't you?" Nico countered.

"Nico, you ever noticed how the director will sit in the background, right behind the screen, crafting his story? He'll call *cut* countless times to make sure he gets it all together, and to his liking, his perfection!" I said as Nico nodded.

"Even after he's finished, edited, cut out the parts he doesn't like, I mean watched it over and over maybe a hundred times. You ever noticed how he knows he's watched it over a hundred times, he still shows up to the movie premier. He doesn't go to the movie premiere to watch the movie for the umpteenth time. He goes to watch everyone's faces, their reactions." I explained. Nico smiled, but I didn't think he understood what I meant.

"See, I just came to see their faces. To see their reaction. I got Angel's, and now I have to get Kendrick's. But first, I have to pay a visit to Luis.

"Will I be going with you?" Nico asked.

"Nah, you stay here with Angel. I'll take Ron's freaky ass with me. Can't leave him with her. She might not have any clothes on when we get back. Matter of fact, tell him to get the car, we're leaving in twenty!" I instructed.

"Sure thing, boss," Nico said.

As Nico went to attend to business, I took a seat and poured myself a glass of Cognac. It had been a while since I last took a drive to Luis' house. Each time it had always been on a business note. Laughs, drinks, a peaceful business arrangement. This time would be different. This time I had to show my face, to let him know that I was alive. But, I had to let him know his longtime, most trusted soldier was dead. I had exited the game on my own terms. Now I was forced to come back in. And this time, the game wasn't the same. The rules had changed. And my opposition was my own blood. A man that I had taught everything I knew to.

I smiled as I downed the shot of Cognac. This was going to be one hell of a war.

———

Nico

"RON, OG SAID—" I began to say as I opened the door where Ron and Angel were. As I walked in, Ron was standing in front of Angel, caressing her cheek with the back of his hand. Now, I knew why Turtle had Ron around, but I disliked the creepy bastard. Ron was a hard core freak, and I meant that in every way. Ron had alone twenty-eight years in the feds, flat time. Locked up, he had become a hard man. Cold-hearted. Before he went to the feds, he used to run with my pops, and Turtle. So once he got out, they pulled him in, and gave him a job. Ron wasn't just a shooter; Ron was more of a torturer. He took joy in inflicting pain on people. He didn't have any lines that he didn't cross. My pops once told me a story of how this one so-called tough guy had owed Turtle for ten kilos back in the day, the guy thought he was stiff, a tough guy. Ron got him tied him up to a tree and raped him. Yeah, I know, he was a sicko, but that's why he got paid. But that was also why I kept a close eye on him when I was around him.

"Ron, come on, man. Turtle said he needs you to take a trip with him to Luis. He said get the car ready. He'll meet you at the car in like twenty minutes."

Ron looked at me a little disappointed. He huffed and looked back to Angel and said, "Don't go anywhere. I'll be back later." Ron walked off, but stopped as he stood beside me. He smiled then said, "She looks good, huh? I think she tastes better than she looks." Rico laughed, drawing an even more disgusting opinion about him from me. He patted me on the back and said, "Have fun!"

I shook my head as he walked out the room. That man really gave me the creeps. I didn't understand his tactics one bit. I grabbed the abandoned wooden chair and pulled it to the wall across from Angel. I leaned back to get comfortable as I pulled my Glock from my hip and laid it across my top.

I looked over to Angel; her chest rose and fell at a slow pace. I remembered what Ron said. She did look good, despite her busted lip and swollen eye. Deep under her trauma and pain, I could see her beauty. I could see her walking the streets turning heads. I could also see her on Ken's arms. His wife, his ride-or-die bitch. His world. My old best friend.

"Arghh!" Angel groaned painfully as she stirred in her restraints. Her head rose as she looked around with her good eye. As she surveyed the room, her eyes landed on me. She froze. "You're on baby-sitting duty?" she asked.

"I wouldn't call you a baby, but I am on sitting duty," I said as I sat up in my chair.

"So, what's the dos and don'ts?" she asked.

"Meaning?"

"I mean, can a bitch go to the bathroom, or do I have to pee on myself? Can a bitch have some water, or do I have to drink my spit?" she asked.

"As of now, my orders are to leave you tied up until Turtle says different."

"So you're telling me a bitch is going to die with a pissy pussy. Ha!" She laughed.

I pulled my phone from my pocket and sent a text to Turtle seeing if bathroom privileges were permitted. He texted back with one word, *cautiously*. He didn't need to tell me that I knew Angel was considered a dangerous flight risk.

"You're in luck," I said as I stood up. I placed my phone back in my pocket and walked behind Angel.

"My luck hasn't been so good as of lately," she said. I laughed. I grabbed Ron's pliers and walked back around to Angel's feet, I kneeled in front of her and cut the zip tie with the pliers. Angel moved her legs like she had been tied up for years. I helped her stand with the rope that was tied to her hands.

"Thank you," she said with a smile. "Now, what about my hands?" she said as she looked into my eyes.

"It don't get that good. Now the bathroom is right there. I'ma wait for you out here!" I said as she just looked at me. "What is it now?" I asked.

"How am I supposed to pee with these pants on? I can pull my own thong off, but damn, how can I unbutton my pants with my hands tied up behind my back?"

I knew what she was asking, but I was told to keep her hands tied up, and I was against disobeying orders. "Angel, I'm not about to untie your hands, so what's next?"

She walked up to me and said, "Then you're going to have to take my pants off for me."

It felt like I had a lump in my throat as I tried to swallow my spit. I wasn't a virgin or nothing like that, so I don't even know why I was nervous. Then again I don't even know why I was tripping; it wasn't like I was about to fuck her, just take her clothes off. Who was I kidding, I knew why I was nervous. Angel was something serious. She wasn't the most beautiful woman I've ever seen but her presence was at a level I've never seen from a woman.

I sighed. "Don't try nothing," I said as I kneeled in front of her.

Angel laughed. "What am I going to do, rub my pussy in your face, make you suffocate to death? Boy, begone." She laughed. Even though I wasn't supposed to, I found myself laughing. I had to catch myself, getting a more serious face as I reached for her pants. I took a slow deep breath as I unbuttoned her pants, then unzipped them. I stopped, then looked up at her.

"Now take them off," she said.

"All the way?"

"Duh!" she said, looking down on me.

I stuck my thumb in her waistband and started pulling her pants down. Her pants got stuck around her ass. I wrapped my thumb around her backside, my finger brushing against her thumb. I pulled her pants down as they fell to her ankles.

I looked behind me, then back to the front of me. It was like I had been teleported to the Sahara Desert or something. Like I was in India. Angel's camel toe was looking me directly in the eye. I found myself taking a deep breath, inhaling her scent. She smelled good. Her scent was intoxicating. I had to regain my composure. Pussy only had power when you gave it power. I looked in Angel's eyes as I placed my left hand on her waistline. I held her waist for her own support. "Raise your left leg," I demanded. Angel raised her left leg as she returned my stare. I stood and pointed to the bathroom.

"Seat is already up. I'll be out here!" I said.

"One more thing," Angel said as she stood before me with just a black shirt and a black thong on.

"What now?" I asked, trying hard to be stiff, showing her that her sexy, tight body wasn't affecting me. Knowing deep down it did.

"Can you pull my thong down under my ass, please." She begged.

I know what she was trying to do. She was trying to use her looks, her goodies to get to me. To harden places that had no self-control. But I held my own. I wasn't going to let a piece of pussy weaken me. And I was never going to be the weak link in the chain. So I did what I had to do. I mean, I did what any man in my position was supposed to do. I showed her dick was stronger than pussy.

I stood before Angel, looking directly in her eyes. I reached out my hand to her thong. Instead of pulling them down I hooked my finger in the seat of her thong, my finger brushing against her sex lips. As I looked deep into her eyes, I noticed hers had slowly began to close. I pulled her thong just a tad, then I moved it over, exposing her sex lips to view. Without looking down, I took a step back and walked away. Once Angel finally opened her eyes to realize her tactic didn't work, I was sitting in the same seat she had just been tied up in. As she noticed me in the chair, she huffed with a deep breath, then sighed.

"You're tougher than I thought," she said as she walked towards the bathroom. She didn't have to tell me that; I already knew I was. At least for now I was.

29

TURTLE

It had been a very long time since I was last here. But the place still looked the same. The only thing Luis changed about his estate was the gardening. But he still kept the same workers he always had. Luis was like me in so many ways. He didn't trust many, and he always kept a close eye on the ones he did trust.

"Boss, do they know we're here?" Ron asked.

"They know. Just be patient!" I said as I waited for someone to exit the front door to invite us in. Luis knew I was here. I had phoned him hours before to inform him of my visit. I just wasn't able to go into too much detail over the phone. After another two or three minutes, the front door opened, and we were invited in. "Ron, don't speak unless you're spoken to, just stand on the side of me, and stay quiet," I instructed as we exited the car.

"Sure thing, boss."

Lluvia

My father made all of the chefs prepare a huge feast like the king of Zamunda was coming. To me, Turtle was just another one of my father's day associates, but my father treated Turtle like family, like a brother. I had nothing against Turtle. I gave him favor for taking Kendrick in, and raising him as his own. I just didn't like how Turtle left Kendrick for dead during his entire trial. Even though Kendrick didn't see me face to face, I was at his trial, sitting way in the back like a news reporter.

See, I held Kendrick. Always have, and I always would. He held a place in my heart no man could fill. As bad as it felt in my heart to think about it, we shared a son together. And no matter what the paperwork says, I will never let our son die.

"Luis, this place looks great and what is that I smell? Is it Thanksgiving and I didn't know it?" Turtle said as my father and him embraced.

"You know a visit from you calls for special occasions. Here, sit. Let us pour ourselves a glass for your safe return home."

Hiding in the other room like a sneaky child, I listened in on everything. It's been like that since I was a kid.

Turtle cleared his throat and said, "Luis, I just want to thank you for what you sacrificed for me. Believe me, I will repay you."

My father held up his glass. "To brotherhood."

"To brotherhood," Turtle said as they toasted.

Turtle sat his glass down. My father refilled both of

theirs. I came all this way to thank you, and also to tell you face to face that . . . Filipe didn't make it."

My father paused for a second, then he raised his glass again. "To Filipe." He toasted.

"To Filipe," Turtle said as he downed his drink. Filipe's loss was a painful one. I knew it hurt my father; he just was good at hiding his emotions. Filipe's been in our family's circle since I was a little girl. He was my father's right-hand man and my second father.

My father downed his drink, then sat the glass down on the table. "What of
Angel? Did she—"

Turtle hung his head and shook it slowly. "She didn't make it. Filipe died protecting her. They both died with great honor!" Turtle said as he scooted to the edge of his seat. "Before Angel took her last breath, she spoke on some property you gave her to exchange for me, but she didn't disclose the location. I wanted to come to you and tell you face to face, I will find it, and return it to you, with interest."

"That's a huge burden you're putting on yourself, Turtle. I wouldn't expect you to put that on your shoulders. You've done nothing wrong. I knew what could happen when I sent Filipe to help, and I knew I could lose the shipment. It's all a part of the game. I'm just glad you're back."

I turned my back to the wall and took a deep breath. It pained me to see Kendrick going through so many losses. He's been taking them one after the other. To have lost a son, then when Turtle got out the drug game, and started dealing with politicians, it was like Kendrick had lost an uncle too. Now to be in prison, and have to receive the news of him losing his wife too. So many losses like that could drive even the strongest man to his knees.

I hurried towards the back door to make a quick escape. I figured if anyone was to tell Kendrick of the bad news, it had to be me.

———

Emmanuel

THE ONE RULE about being a criminal was: you never returned to the scene where you committed the crime. But in this case I had no other choice. And even though I wasn't the killer, I was guilty by association. There was a lot that I wish I could change about the last few months of my life. First, I would've handled Kendrick's case a different way. I would've never let Angel dangle money in my face to where she got me to go with her to get some money I knew damn well I wasn't supposed to receive without a money order. Secondly, I wish I had paid more attention to my wife, Hannah. If I had loved her more, and worked less, maybe she would still be here. Then I think about Janice, and the love I now have for her. It's crazy how *bad* works. You could work right beside someone for years, and never know how much you actually love them.

"Manny, are you okay?" Janice asked, bringing me back to reality. A reality I wasn't quite sure I wanted to be in.

I nodded as I looked at the spot on the floor that was hours before the section for my rug. The same rug we rolled Squirrel's body in just before we tossed him in the trunk of Bull's car.

I stepped over a puddle of blood as I grabbed the stair rail. Even though I had been up these steps countless times, this time would be the first since Hannah took her last breath. I imagined Janice would be behind me, but as I looked behind me, I didn't imagine Janice would be in tears.

I stopped at the top of the stairs and pulled Janice to me. "Shh-hh. Everything's going to be okay." I consoled her.

"We both know I wasn't fond of her, but she didn't deserve to die, and she didn't deserve to die like that. An- And the baby." Janice bawled her eyes out.

I squeezed Janice close to me tightly. My chin rested on the top of her head as I fought as hard as I could to prevent myself from crying as well. "We can't change what happened, but we can make sure she gets justice," I assured her.

"So," Janice began to say as she wiped her eyes. "Do you really think this is going to work?"

"It should," I said as we walked in the bedroom. "I just hope he lets me see him. If I was him, I wouldn't want to see me either."

"We have to be quick. There's no telling if the police were able to tie her to you yet, so we have to do this quickly," Janice said.

"I know, we need to shower, and change clothes first. We can't go up there looking like this." I looked at all the blood and dirt all over our clothes.

"What am I to wear?" she asked.

"Pick something from Hannah's old clothes. Sad to say, she doesn't need them anymore."

30

BIG KEN

"Family, sit down man. You going to walk the cement out the floor." Slim laughed, causing Blip and Los to laugh as well. I ignored them like I was the only person in the room. I continued my slow, deep-thought pace as I walked around the small cell back and forth with my hands behind my back.

I held Slim's phone in my hand as I continued to pace. I just wasn't understanding this. Angel went to deliver the ki's a day ago, and she hasn't checked in. Pistol told me how Bishop and his crew had been found dead in the car shop. Bishop with a bullet in his forehead. If I'm guessing right, Luis sent a clean-up crew to gather his soldiers because it was only the Bishop's crew found. What I couldn't understand was where was Angel and my uncle Turtle. I would've checked Angel's Instagram, one thing she couldn't live without, but Slim's old flip phone didn't have the app.

"Kendrick Watson!" the guard said, startling me. I tucked Slim's phone under my arm.

"What's up? I'm Watson!" I said nervously.

"You have a visit, go get ready, I'll be back in five minutes."

As the CO started to walk away, I stopped him. I didn't need five minutes to get dressed. I was as ready as I'll ever be. Hell, it wasn't like I had a helluva wardrobe to choose from.

"Let's go, boss, ain't no need to waste time." The CO nodded as he used his single key to open the door. I placed my hands behind my back, thinking I was to be cuffed and escorted. Once the CO told me which direction to go, to keep my hands behind my back as I followed him in his directions, I complied.

"Do you know who's here for me?" I asked, curiously.

"Not sure of the name, but I can say it's a woman and, if I can say, a beautiful one at that."

Once the words left his mouth, my mind instantly went to Angel. I just knew it was her. The CO pointed towards an entrance. I walked in the room and looked around with a big smile on my face. I scanned the first row of visitors, and neither were Angel. I kept up my search, and my eyes landed on a familiar face, but it wasn't Angel.

"Lluvia, what are you doing here?" I asked as I pulled the chair out and took a seat.

"Wow!" Lluvia said with an irritated look.

"Good to see you Rain, thank you for coming, Rain, how are you Rain?" she said, sarcastically.

"I-I'm sorry—it's just." I sighed, then said, "I just thought you were—" I stopped mid-sentence.

"I know I'm not your precious Angel!" Lluvia said a little loud.

"I didn't mean it like that, Rain." I sighed.

"I got a lot going on as you can see. I only thought you were Angel because I had her make a run for me, and no one has heard from her."

"That's why I'm here," Lluvia said.

"What do you mean?" I asked. "Did someone send you to see me?"

My question caused Rain to cock her head to the side. She looked at me like she was upset about something. "No! No one had me come down here. I came on my own." She huffed.

I stayed silent to let her gather her thoughts. I knew coming down here was a lot for her. Once she relaxed, she said, "This is going to be hard for me to say, Kendrick."

My mind instantly went negative. I jumped to my feet. "Is it Angel or Turtle? Are they okay?" I shouted. One of the guards began to walk in my direction.

"Take a seat, and lower your voice, or I'll be forced to terminate your visit." I ignored the guard as I placed both fists on the table, my knuckles pressed hard on the table.

"Sir!" the guard said.

I looked at him. I was seconds away from doing him the same way I did my lawyer. As I clenched my jaw tighter, Rain grabbed my arm, calming me briefly. Just by her touch I was able to think straight. I took my seat and prepared myself for what was to come.

The guard walked off like he had won. I let him think that I had some serious shit going on. As soon as the guard walked away, I looked at Rain and said: "I know you didn't come all this way to make me guess. So tell me what the fuck is going on."

Lluvia moved the hair out in front of her face and said, "Your uncle is okay," then she paused. I knew when she paused, there was a 'but' coming next! Lluvia sighed before she continued, "But your wife, Angel."

My eyes closed at the mention of Angel's name. I knew I shouldn't have let her go. Whatever happened to her was my fault.

"What-what happened to her?" I asked.

"She was killed!" Lluvia said, sadly. I heard every word that came out of her mouth, but it somehow seemed like my ears had all of a sudden stopped working. Like my mind was trying to unhear what it just heard. I hadn't cried in so long; it felt weird to feel the fluid coming down my face. I wiped my eyes to try to get the tears to stop, but they wouldn't

"So, you're telling me that my wife, Angel, is no longer walking this earth. That my wife is no longer here. The woman that promised to hold me down through this bid, the woman that promised me for better or worse. You're sitting here in my face, telling me that I'll never ever see her smile again. That we will never be able to hold each other again." Lluvia was in tears as she sat across from me. She had never seen me cry before. She was at a loss for words as she wiped her tears away.

"Who told you?" I asked.

"Who told me what?" she asked, her voice cracking.

"Who told you my wife was dead?" I asked.

"No one told me personally. I overheard Turtle telling my father, and I came straight here to tell you."

"How did he make it out alive?" I asked, curiously

"I don't know, he didn't say!" she said. My mind was all over the place. I was doing things in my mind that brought the strongest armies no defect. I was mourning while planning my revenge. A trainer calls it fighting out of emotion. A big no-no.

"Who all survived, did you hear?" I questioned.

"From what Turtle said, it was just him. Even Filipe died."

"So, Bishop got away with killing my wife, and with two hundred ki's."

"No, he's dead too. From what Turtle said, he was the only survivor, and Angel never brought the ki's, so no one knows where they are."

Something just wasn't adding up to me. Really, none of it was. For one, it didn't sit right with me that my own uncle, my flesh and blood didn't come to tell me on his own that my wife died trying to save him. And then, no one knew where the ki's were, none of it made any sense.

I cleared my throat and stood up. "Do me a favor, contact Pistol, tell him to pull up, like yesterday," I instructed.

Rain nodded as she stood up. "What are you thinking?" she asked. Rain knew me well. Once before, she was my Angel. She was my ride-or-die, my right hand, my better half. So she knew when shit was going crazy in my mind, like now.

"Too early to say, but I will say that what you heard wasn't the truth." I opened my arms as Rain walked into my embrace. I held her and caressed her back. "Get that message out for me, and I'll call you later." She nodded as she looked at me.

My demeanor had changed. I couldn't go back to the dorm all sad and down. This was the big house, and I had to remember in the big house, only the strong were able to eat. The weak were preyed upon. I turned and walked away without looking back. I knew if I would've looked back, the pain would've all come rushing back.

The short walk back to my dorm gave me just enough time to clear my mind. Once I got to the dorm, the same guard that escorted me to visitation called my name.

"Watson!"

I looked back and said, "Yeah, wassup?"

"You have another visit," the guard said.

"I thought we could only have one per weekend?" I asked to be sure.

"Yes, but this is an attorney visit."

31

EMMANUEL

I told Janice to wait in the car as I decided to do the right thing. So much has happened in the past week. Life-changing events, one after the other. I had done a lot of wrong in my life. And being a defense attorney was one of them. Every client I ever took was guilty, but I still accepted their money. Kendrick was no different. He was guilty. But that didn't mean he didn't deserve a fair trial. When I parked outside, Janice pleaded with me to do the right thing. She insisted that we should just leave, and never look back. She said that Kendrick marrying a snake wasn't my fault. But in my mind. In my heart it was. Because I let the snake bite him, knowing I could've warned him. Janice even said that Kendrick would deny my visit. I thought about that too, but I had turned my back on him; it was only fair that I let him turn his back on me. My head was low as Kendrick walked in the room. Once I heard him, I looked up. It sucked knowing I was a man, but I was unable to look him in the eyes.

"You got some nerve, showing up here after you fucked me over!" Kendrick said as stood behind his chair.

"I know, but if you would just let me explain, please."

Kendrick laughed at my words. "Nigga, fuck you! You lucky I don't choke yo' ass out and let them crackas add it to my already life sentence." Kendrick shook his head in anger. He turned his back and grabbed the doorknob.

"Wait!" I said. "It's about your wife, Angel."

To Be Continued...

Assisted Publishing Packages

BASIC PACKAGE

$699

Editing

Cover Design

Formatting

UPGRADED PACKAGE

$1,000

Typing

Editing

Cover Design

Formatting

ADVANCE PACKAGE

$1,400

Typing

Editing

Cover Design

Formatting

Copyright registration

Proofreading

Upload book to Amazon

LDP SUPREME PACKAGE

$1,700

Typing

Editing

Cover Design

Formatting

Copyright registration

Proofreading

Set up Amazon account

Upload book to Amazon

Advertise on LDP, Amazon and Facebook Page

Submission Guidelines

Submit the first three chapters of your completed manuscript to ldpsubmissions@gmail.com. In the subject line add Your Book's Title. The manuscript must be in a Word Doc file and sent as an attachment. Document should be in Times New Roman, double spaced, and in size 12 font. Also, provide your synopsis and full contact information. If sending multiple submissions, they must each be in a separate email.

Have a story but no way to send it electronically? You can still submit to LDP/Ca$h Presents. Send in the first three chapters, written or typed, of your completed manuscript to:

LDP: Submissions Dept
P.O. Box 944
Stockbridge, GA 30281-9998

DO NOT send original manuscript. Must be a duplicate.
Provide your synopsis and a cover letter containing your full contact information.

Thanks for considering LDP and Ca$h Presents.

NEW RELEASES

BLOODLINE OF A SAVAGE 1&2
THESE VICIOUS STREETS 1&2
RELENTLESS GOON
RELENTLESS GOON 2
BY PRINCE A. TAUHID

THE BUTTERFLY MAFIA 1-3
BY FUMIYA PAYNE

A THUG'S STREET PRINCESS 1&2
BY MEESHA

CITY OF SMOKE 2
BY MOLOTTI

STEPPERS 1,2&3
THE REAL BADDIES OF CHI-RAQ
BY KING RIO

THE LANE 1&2
BY KEN-KEN SPENCE

THUG OF SPADES 1&2
LOVE IN THE TRENCHES 2
CORNER BOYS
BY COREY ROBINSON

TIL DEATH 3

BY ARYANNA

THE BIRTH OF A GANGSTER 4
BY DELMONT PLAYER

PRODUCT OF THE STREETS 1&2
BY DEMOND "MONEY" ANDERSON

NO TIME FOR ERROR
BY KEESE

MONEY HUNGRY DEMONS
BY TRANAY ADAMS

STANDING ON HER BUSINESS 2
BY DG SANTANA

TENDER
BY KHUFU

HUB CITY MENACE
BY JAQUILLE M. WHITE

COUNTDOWN TO A KILLA
CLOCK'S TICKING
BY LO-LIFE

FO'EVA ROLLIN'
BY ASSA RAYMOND BAKER

THUG OF SPADES 3

BY COREY ROBINSON

THE PLUG'S RUTHLESS DAUGHTER 2
BY TONY DANIELS

DYING FOR LIKES
KILLING AIN'T A GAME
BY ARYANNA

GET IT IN SLUGS
BY B STALL

BLOODY MONEY BAGS
VIOLENT LOVE
BY KINGPEN

Coming Soon from Lock Down Publications/Ca$h Presents

IF YOU CROSS ME ONCE 6
ANGEL V
By Anthony Fields

IMMA DIE BOUT MINE 5
By Aryanna

A THUGS STREET PRINCESS 3
By Meesha

PRODUCT OF THE STREETS 3
By Demond Money Anderson

CORNER BOYS 2
By Corey Robinson

THE MURDER QUEENS 6&7
By Michael Gallon

CITY OF SMOKE 3
By Molotti

CONFESSIONS OF A DOPE BOY
By Nicholas Lock

THA TAKEOVER
By Keith Chandler

BETRAYAL OF A G 2
By Ray Vinci

CRIME BOSS
By Playa Ray

Available Now

RESTRAINING ORDER 1 & 2
By CA$H & Coffee

LOVE KNOWS NO BOUNDARIES 1-3
By Coffee

RAISED AS A GOON I, II, III & IV
BRED BY THE SLUMS I, II, III
BLAST FOR ME I & II
ROTTEN TO THE CORE I II III
A BRONX TALE I, II, III
DUFFLE BAG CARTEL I II III IV V VI
HEARTLESS GOON I II III IV V
A SAVAGE DOPEBOY I II
DRUG LORDS I II III
CUTTHROAT MAFIA I II
KING OF THE TRENCHES
By Ghost

LAY IT DOWN I & II
LAST OF A DYING BREED I II
BLOOD STAINS OF A SHOTTA I & II III
By Jamaica

LOYAL TO THE GAME I II III
LIFE OF SIN I, II III
By TJ & Jelissa

IF LOVING HIM IS WRONG…I & II
LOVE ME EVEN WHEN IT HURTS I II III
By Jelissa

PUSH IT TO THE LIMIT
By Bre' Hayes

BLOODY COMMAS I & II
SKI MASK CARTEL I, II & III
KING OF NEW YORK I II, III IV V
RISE TO POWER I II III
COKE KINGS I II III IV V
BORN HEARTLESS I II III IV
KING OF THE TRAP I II
By T.J. Edwards

WHEN THE STREETS CLAP BACK I & II III
THE HEART OF A SAVAGE I II III IV
MONEY MAFIA I II
LOYAL TO THE SOIL I II III
By Jibril Williams

A DISTINGUISHED THUG STOLE MY HEART I
II & III
LOVE SHOULDN'T HURT I II III IV
RENEGADE BOYS 1-4
PAID IN KARMA 1-3

SAVAGE STORMS 1-3
AN UNFORESEEN LOVE 1-3
BABY, I'M WINTERTIME COLD 1-3
A THUG'S STREET PRINCESS 1&2
By Meesha

A GANGSTER'S CODE 1-3
A GANGSTER'S SYN 1-3
THE SAVAGE LIFE 1-3
CHAINED TO THE STREETS 1-3
BLOOD ON THE MONEY 1-3
A GANGSTA'S PAIN 1-3
BEAUTIFUL LIES AND UGLY TRUTHS
CHURCH IN THESE STREETS
By J-Blunt

CUM FOR ME 1-8
An LDP Erotica Collaboration

BLOOD OF A BOSS 1-5
SHADOWS OF THE GAME
TRAP BASTARD
By Askari

THE STREETS BLEED MURDER 1-3
THE HEART OF A GANGSTA 1-3
By Jerry Jackson

WHEN A GOOD GIRL GOES BAD
By Adrienne

THE COST OF LOYALTY 1-3
By Kweli

BRIDE OF A HUSTLA 1-3
THE FETTI GIRLS 1-3
CORRUPTED BY A GANGSTA 1-4
BLINDED BY HIS LOVE
THE PRICE YOU PAY FOR LOVE 1-3
DOPE GIRL MAGIC 1-3
By Destiny Skai

A KINGPIN'S AMBITION
A KINGPIN'S AMBITION II
I MURDER FOR THE DOUGH
By Ambitious

TRUE SAVAGE 1-7
DOPE BOY MAGIC 1-3
MIDNIGHT CARTEL 1-3
CITY OF KINGZ 1&2
NIGHTMARE ON SILENT AVE
THE PLUG OF LIL MEXICO 1&2
CLASSIC CITY
By Chris Green

A GANGSTER'S REVENGE 1-4
THE BOSS MAN'S DAUGHTERS 1-5
A SAVAGE LOVE 1&2
BAE BELONGS TO ME 1&2
A HUSTLER'S DECEIT 1-3
WHAT BAD BITCHES DO 1-3

SOUL OF A MONSTER 1-3
KILL ZONE
A DOPE BOY'S QUEEN 1-3
TIL DEATH 1-3
IMMA DIE BOUT MINE 1-4
By Aryanna

A DOPEBOY'S PRAYER
By Eddie "Wolf" Lee

THE KING CARTEL 1-3
By Frank Gresham

THESE NIGGAS AIN'T LOYAL 1-3
By Nikki Tee

GANGSTA SHYT 1-3
By CATO

THE ULTIMATE BETRAYAL
By Phoenix

BOSS'N UP 1-3
By Royal Nicole

I LOVE YOU TO DEATH
By Destiny J

I RIDE FOR MY HITTA
I STILL RIDE FOR MY HITTA
By Misty Holt

LOVE & CHASIN' PAPER
By Qay Crockett

TO DIE IN VAIN
SINS OF A HUSTLA
By ASAD

BROOKLYN HUSTLAZ
By Boogsy Morina

BROOKLYN ON LOCK 1 & 2
By Sonovia

GANGSTA CITY
By Teddy Duke

A DRUG KING AND HIS DIAMOND 1-3
A DOPEMAN'S RICHES
HER MAN, MINE'S TOO 1&2
CASH MONEY HO'S
THE WIFEY I USED TO BE 1&2
PRETTY GIRLS DO NASTY THINGS
By Nicole Goosby

LIPSTICK KILLAH 1-3
CRIME OF PASSION 1-3
FRIEND OR FOE 1-3
By Mimi

TRAPHOUSE KING 1-3
KINGPIN KILLAZ 1-3

STREET KINGS 1&2
PAID IN BLOOD 1&2
CARTEL KILLAZ 1-3
DOPE GODS 1&2
By Hood Rich

THE STREETS ARE CALLING
By Duquie Wilson

STEADY MOBBN' 1-3
THE STREETS STAINED MY SOUL 1-3
By Marcellus Allen

WHO SHOT YA 1-3
SON OF A DOPE FIEND 1-4
HEAVEN GOT A GHETTO 1&2
SKI MASK MONEY 1&2
By Renta

GORILLAZ IN THE BAY 1-4
TEARS OF A GANGSTA 1/&2
3X KRAZY 1&2
STRAIGHT BEAST MODE 1&2
By DE'KARI

TRIGGADALE 1-3
MURDA WAS THE CASE 1-3
By Elijah R. Freeman

SLAUGHTER GANG 1-3
RUTHLESS HEART 1-3

By Willie Slaughter

GOD BLESS THE TRAPPERS 1-3
THESE SCANDALOUS STREETS 1-3
FEAR MY GANGSTA 1-5
THESE STREETS DON'T LOVE NOBODY 1-2
BURY ME A G 1-5
A GANGSTA'S EMPIRE 1-4
THE DOPEMAN'S BODYGAURD 1&2
THE REALEST KILLAZ 1-3
THE LAST OF THE OGS 1-3
By Tranay Adams

MARRIED TO A BOSS 1-3
By Destiny Skai & Chris Green

KINGZ OF THE GAME 1-7
CRIME BOSS 1-3
By Playa Ray

FUK SHYT
By Blakk Diamond

DON'T F#CK WITH MY HEART 1&2
By Linnea

ADDICTED TO THE DRAMA 1-3
IN THE ARM OF HIS BOSS
By Jamila

LOYALTY AIN'T PROMISED 1&2

By Keith Williams

YAYO 1-4
A SHOOTER'S AMBITION 1&2
BRED IN THE GAME
By S. Allen

TRAP GOD 1-3
RICH $AVAGE 1-3
MONEY IN THE GRAVE 1-3
CARTEL MONEY
By Martell Troublesome Bolden

FOREVER GANGSTA 1&2
GLOCKS ON SATIN SHEETS 1&2
By Adrian Dulan

TOE TAGZ 1-4
LEVELS TO THIS SHYT 1&2
IT'S JUST ME AND YOU
By Ah'Million

KINGPIN DREAMS 1-3
RAN OFF ON DA PLUG
By Paper Boi Rari

THE STREETS MADE ME 1-3
By Larry D. Wright

CONFESSIONS OF A GANGSTA 1-4
CONFESSIONS OF A JACKBOY 1-3

CONFESSIONS OF A HITMAN
By Nicholas Lock

I'M NOTHING WITHOUT HIS LOVE
SINS OF A THUG
TO THE THUG I LOVED BEFORE
A GANGSTA SAVED XMAS
IN A HUSTLER I TRUST
By Monet Dragun

QUIET MONEY 1-3
THUG LIFE 1-3
EXTENDED CLIP 1&2
A GANGSTA'S PARADISE
By Trai'Quan

CAUGHT UP IN THE LIFE 1-3
THE STREETS NEVER LET GO 1-3
By Robert Baptiste

NEW TO THE GAME 1-3
MONEY, MURDER & MEMORIES 1-3
By Malik D. Rice

CREAM 2-3
THE STREETS WILL TALK
By Yolanda Moore

THE STREETS WILL NEVER CLOSE 1-3
By K'ajji

LIFE OF A SAVAGE 1-4
A GANGSTA'S QUR'AN 1-4
MURDA SEASON 1-3
GANGLAND CARTEL 1-3
CHI'RAQ GANGSTAS 1-4
KILLERS ON ELM STREET 1-3
JACK BOYZ N DA BRONX 1-3
A DOPEBOY'S DREAM 1-3
JACK BOYS VS DOPE BOYS 1-3
COKE GIRLZ
COKE BOYS
SOSA GANG 1&2
BRONX SAVAGES
BODYMORE KINGPINS
BLOOD OF A GOON
By Romell Tukes

CONCRETE KILLA 1-3
VICIOUS LOYALTY 1-3
By Kingpen

THE ULTIMATE SACRIFICE 1-6
KHADIFI
IF YOU CROSS ME ONCE 1-3
ANGEL 1-4
IN THE BLINK OF AN EYE
By Anthony Fields

THE LIFE OF A HOOD STAR
By Ca$h & Rashia Wilson

NIGHTMARES OF A HUSTLA 1-3
BLOOD AND GAMES 1&2
By King Dream

GHOST MOB
By Stilloan Robinson

HARD AND RUTHLESS 1&2
MOB TOWN 251
THE BILLIONAIRE BENTLEYS 1-3
REAL G'S MOVE IN SILENCE
By Von Diesel

MOB TIES 1-7
SOUL OF A HUSTLER, HEART OF A KILLER 1-3
GORILLAZ IN THE TRENCHES
By SayNoMore

BODYMORE MURDERLAND 1-3
THE BIRTH OF A GANGSTER 1-4
By Delmont Player

FOR THE LOVE OF A BOSS 1&2
By C. D. Blue

KILLA KOUNTY 1-5
By Khufu

MOBBED UP 1-4
THE BRICK MAN 1-5
THE COCAINE PRINCESS 1-10

STEPPERS 1-3
SUPER GREMLIN 1-4
By King Rio

MONEY GAME 1&2
By Smoove Dolla

A GANGSTA'S KARMA 1-4
By FLAME

KING OF THE TRENCHES 1-3
By GHOST & TRANAY ADAMS

QUEEN OF THE ZOO 1&2
By Black Migo

GRIMEY WAYS 1-3
BETRAYAL OF A G
By Ray Vinci

XMAS WITH AN ATL SHOOTER
By Ca$h & Destiny Skai

KING KILLA 1&2
By Vincent "Vitto" Holloway

BETRAYAL OF A THUG 1&2
By Fre$h

THE MURDER QUEENS 1-5
By Michael Gallon

FOR THE LOVE OF BLOOD 1-4
By Jamel Mitchell

HOOD CONSIGLIERE 1&2
NO TIME FOR ERROR
By Keese

PROTÉGÉ OF A LEGEND 1&2
LOVE IN THE TRENCHES 1&2
By Corey Robinson

THE PLUG'S RUTHLESS DAUGHTER
By Tony Daniels

BORN IN THE GRAVE 1-3
CRIME PAYS
By Self Made Tay

MOAN IN MY MOUTH
By XTASY

TORN BETWEEN A GANGSTER AND A
GENTLEMAN
By J-BLUNT & Miss Kim

LOYALTY IS EVERYTHING 1-3
CITY OF SMOKE 1&2
By Molotti

HERE TODAY GONE TOMORROW 1&2
By Fly Rock

WOMEN LIE MEN LIE 1-4
FIFTY SHADES OF SNOW 1-3
STACK BEFORE YOU SPLURGE
GIRLS FALL LIKE DOMINOES
NAÏVE TO THE STREETS
By ROY MILLIGAN

PILLOW PRINCESS
By S. Hawkins

THE BUTTERFLY MAFIA 1-3
SALUTE MY SAVAGERY 1&2
By Fumiya Payne

THE LANE 1&2
By Ken-Ken Spence

THE PUSSY TRAP 1-5
By Nene Capri

DIRTY DNA
By Blaque

SANCTIFIED AND HORNY
by XTASY

BOOKS BY LDP'S CEO, CA$H

TRUST IN NO MAN

TRUST IN NO MAN 2

TRUST IN NO MAN 3

BONDED BY BLOOD

SHORTY GOT A THUG

THUGS CRY

THUGS CRY 2

THUGS CRY 3

TRUST NO BITCH

TRUST NO BITCH 2

TRUST NO BITCH 3

TIL MY CASKET DROPS

RESTRAINING ORDER

RESTRAINING ORDER 2

IN LOVE WITH A CONVICT

LIFE OF A HOOD STAR

XMAS WITH AN ATL SHOOTER